LUCKY
BREAKS

LUCKY BREAKS

Yevgenia Belorusets

Translated from the Russian
by Eugene Ostashevsky

Pushkin Press

Pushkin Press
71–75 Shelton Street
London WC2H 9JQ

Lucly Breaks was first published as *Щасливі падіння*
(*Shchaslivi padinnia*) in 2018 by Ist Publishing (Kharkiv, Ukraine).

The twenty-three images in this edition are from Yevgenia
Belorusets's photographic series *But I Insist: It's Not Even
Yesterday Yet* (2017) and *War in the Park* (2017).

First published by Pushkin Press in 2022

1 3 5 7 9 8 6 4 2

ISBN 13: 978-1-78227-872-6

Typeset by Tetragon, London
Printed and bound by CPI Group (UK) Ltd, Croydon, CR0 4YY

www.pushkinpress.com

CONTENTS

LUCKY
BREAKS

A NOTE BEFORE THE PREFACE

What can't be given up?
   A pencil.
   A city.
   A street.
   You.

What can't be measured?
   My smile.
   Your concern.
   Our mutual misunderstanding.

What do I believe in?
   I believe nobody can believe in anything definite. It even makes no sense to try. People only make-believe they believe.

When the protagonist of a photography project I worked
on from 2016 to 2018 in East Ukraine—a woman who
was also its participant and coauthor—started this word
game, it impressed me as a most fitting image and photograph of her.

Separated from visual representation, written down in
the form of consecutive lines of text, the game both stood
witness to reality and invited me into it.

You are reading a collection of tales that aspire to a certain
quality of photography: the quality of escaping the author's
final control over the materiality of past events, encounters,
conversations, histories. When I take photographs, I do
not set for myself the goal of creating rows of images by
means of technology, as Vilém Flusser defines photography. Rather, I am more interested in working with memories— the possibility of forming memories with the help
of a photograph that claims to be true despite remaining
someone's fiction, a theatrical contrivance merely based
on everyday life.

All my previous photographic and textual work tried
to capture some aspect of the historical reality of Ukraine
that, for all its scale and significance, remains in shadow,
unseen.

The storylines of *Lucky Breaks*, two of which are
photographic, do not represent the pivotal moments in
the country's present history but—one might think from
a cursory glance—only what occurs on the sidelines. More
precisely, they focus on the deep penetration of traumatic
historical events into the fantasies and experiences of
everyday life.

At least three separate themes, indirectly related to the conflict in East Ukraine, deal not with the conflict itself, but with the surmounting of the conflict through a dialectical process—by means of phantasmagoria, narrative, conversation, and the disclosure of certain situations to the viewer.

The insignificant and the small, the accidental, the superfluous, the repressed—all of these things attract my attention because they will never turn into the trophies that Walter Benjamin talks about in "On the Concept of History": The trophies that winners carry from the present into the future so that they might lay down their booty, like bricks, to construct the dominant historical narrative.

Readers can decide for themselves if the documentation presented here (of the times, conditions, emotions, worldviews) disrupts the language of fiction, a language that over and over proves reductive and resistant to reality.

In this book, the voices of different people resonate and clash; photographs and words also collide, neither given the chance to explain or to illustrate the other. Their interlocked coexistence doesn't allow any one idea, any one voice—especially the author's—to dominate.

One of the two photographic series in this volume continues, in black-and-white, the photographic work I carried out over several years in the mines in East Ukraine, which are still in operation, although located in the conflict zone. Yet this particular short series was shot in peaceful Novovolynsk, a city in the west, near the border of Poland, where an industrial culture similar to that of the Donbas survives and evolves. This book represents the recent history of this culture by images that indicate something evasive but do not name it.

With these photographic sequences and stories I want to show how collisions of different contexts inform and transform the manufacture of narratives, resulting in the rejection of any instruments of certainty.

The woman whose words opened this note will appear in these pages. It will be utterly impossible to recognize her, as her manner of speech has become the foundation for my own.

PREFACE

INTERVIEW (THE JAWS OF FATE)

I have been working on a preface for this book for many months now. What I wanted, above all, was a scientific approach. I planned to concisely set forth some facts about documentality and to deliver, if not the definitive, then a suitably severe verdict against it, only to employ a certain rhetorical maneuver and finally—citing the spot-on remark of a woman I know—to resolve once and for all why topicality is infinitely better than documentality, but not in every respect.

I must admit that, after countless ruminations and epiphanies hazardously abutting despair, but without crossing over into despair proper, I managed to create a preface that was hard to tear your eyes away from. My hands tremble even now when I recall that specimen of significance so magnificently caparisoned.

In the roar of the predawn highway an alcoholic over-
hears a remote chime that people in our parts call "the
snap of the jaws of fate." Its inaccessible beauty evokes
the rhythm I had constructed in that text.

Yet, if you think about it long enough, the role of a
preface will turn out to be too narrow and undeservedly
cramped for an utterance of such caliber. It is an utterance
that ought to aim higher. It must serve as the foundation
for everything else, yet it itself should not be made public
by any means. (Publication is a false target!)

Nor may it be put up for sale. It may perhaps be
bartered for cultural values or handed out as an encouragement for those who are at least partially full, while
those who are hungry might receive it as a momentary
distraction from thoughts of sustenance. Yet lately I had
an occasion to test out the said preface: it did not distract

me, alas, it did not distract me. In one of the coming
chapters I will make sure to return to the notable experience I acquired thereby, so that it can be described in
great detail.

But I cannot pass over in silence an incident that befell
me not long ago—as a matter of fact, just yesterday.

Our neighborhood is quite badly off, although from far
away it appears fairly up to par—maybe even the best-off
neighborhood in Kyiv. But I can tell that its façades of
well-being hide profound and sincere ill-being. Yet how
can something hidden remain sincere? No doubt it cannot.
Still, the earnestness of this ill-being will stun anyone who
dares to discover it. And yet, even here one must be honest
with oneself and recognize how rare in our society is the
daring that the discovery calls for!

So it is no surprise that I felt disconcerted yesterday
evening when, at the entrance to my building—where
someone had screwed out and carried off the bulb that
used to dimly illuminate the small area around the steps
up to the doorway—I discovered first a long shadow,
and then a figure that had separated from a wall awash
in darkness and was menacingly extending an enormous
hand in my direction.

The voice of the person who spoke to me turned out
to be soft and pleasant. A high, melodic voice inhibited
by a tender, impulsive intonation. A woman stood before
me, trying to explain something. She had been wanting
to meet me for a long while now in order to ask me a few
questions.

"Maybe I can cook up some semblance of an interview
from your answers," she nervously suggested. "But it's

more likely that I will fail. I have to confess that I fail at much of what I set out to do. Practically all of my plans, desires, intentions, and goals run aground and go under. But you will kindly spare a few minutes of your time to answer my questions. Believe me, it's not so difficult to answer, especially when the questions are already there in your hands. To formulate the questions—my responsibility completely—is the far more demanding task."

I couldn't help but invite her in for a cup of coffee and hear out her questions, which troubled me before they were even asked. The fact is that any Ukrainian journalist, especially if she, for some unclear reason, displays an interest in art and literature, tends, as a rule, merely to abuse her freedom—and to do so in the most disgraceful manner. But since my marvelously composed preface had by then been disposed of, beyond recovery and retrieval, I was hoping that a brief conversation with an unknown journalist would prod me toward a fresh group of thoughts that I could then set forth before the other texts as an equivalent to a preface. I did understand perfectly well that a dialogue such as this wouldn't touch upon any aspect of the themes and questions that must be elucidated—or at least brought up—in an actual preface to a book such as this. Yet I had no other choice.

Because my initial preface turned out to be unfit for publication, you see, I also had to forego the book's former title, as educational and deeply meaningful as it was. The original title was:

A History of Taxation.

And then, on the next page:

Fragment from a Study of the Early History of Mankind.
I will certainly never be able to think of a better title—
that's clear. "A history of taxation" encompasses not only
all forms of human life but also those enjoyed by the
representatives of the animal world, combining literary
experimentation and scientific reliability within a single
verbal image. Moreover, "the early history of mankind"
narrows and focuses the book's contents on the history
of my country, for it is precisely here, in this place, that
the history of any kind of mankind can find its origin.

But what else was I to do? How could I, despite suffering such palpable losses, let events completely escape the
sphere of my control, that is to say drop the reins, loosen
the grip, let the book go without a title? A thousand ideas
were rushing through my mind, but then I overheard a
soft, alluringly remote sound go off in their torrent.

"You're not saying anything," Andrea began. "I, meanwhile, am starting to suspect that you decided to speak to me out of pity, whereas you actually believe that our conversation won't lead anywhere. And that confirms my fears, because, as I had already confessed, the majority of my intentions and even actions lead nowhere. I write for small regional papers that no one in Kyiv has ever heard of. *North Donetsk News* declines my articles one after another. And they have the right to do so, since I formerly wrote for *Alchevsk Vespers*, *The Lights*, and some other papers that also almost always declined my articles and proposals. After numerous discussions and rejections, I decided to pitch a regular column to *The Dispatches* to be called 'The Diary of a Former Alchie' but they declined this, too, without hearing my full pitch because to them the column's title would be misconstrued by readers, thereby casting a shadow on the whole paper.

"What am I supposed to do," she continued, "if basically no one reads the articles I write? I've started to think that I've never written for any newspapers, that I never could have been able to write anything. I observe things, yes—that I'm good at, even magnificent. But as for writing, I don't really know how to do it, nor do I really want to do it. I refuse to study this art, or craft, whose foundations repose on lies, self-delusion, and blind error.

"As for you"—she would not let me get a word in edgewise—"I see you sitting inside your cozy little apartment, content with yourself, living the life of Riley or else dashing off one thing after another with enviable diligence, calculating, fitting one word to the next, certainly without feeling the uselessness, the senselessness, of what you're

doing, or plotting. You don't need to be afraid of me!
Consider the facts! You had the chance but you didn't
take it. And worse: day by day, week by week you were
becoming encrusted, you even reached the point—and this
makes me recoil in disgust—of 'believing in yourself,' so
to speak! And now you count on me. You're expecting
that I—a person entirely unknown to you, a person who
has lived through so much, who has experienced so much
more than you—that I, myself, and no one else, will present
you with questions I had prepared earlier, questions that
cost me sleepless nights of formulations which I tried to
iron out even while sleeping, or even while helping my
little daughter with her homework! Some nice reckoning
you got there! You're anticipating, with your hideous,
nauseating naiveté, that I would come clean, spill my
questions, and let you again start impudently producing
your so-called answers—so that you may again swim out
into the unknown and paddle back with a verdict you will
remain *satisfied* with!

"You're trying to get away? It's no use! I too was
trying to get away, to ride away, to move to Lviv, or to
Kyiv, to anywhere else. But you can't get away. There's
a moment when cars stop driving out of town, and later
you find out that commuter buses and jitney vans haven't
been running for a long time, and then it dawns on you
that you have remained forever where, in fact, you had
been lingering merely in order to leave that place at some
decisive moment. You are now stuck, you've become a
hostage, a prisoner of people and circumstances, just like
in the movies you used to watch, except that now you've
become an unwilling actor in that movie, only to discover,

to your astonishment, that there isn't and never was an art more petty, more heartless than contemporary cinema, all contemporary cinema without exception, including of course documentaries. Because when you wake up inside a work of whatever genre—comedic, heroic, documentary, military—the movie, to your astonishment, turns out to be unmoving, an infinitely protracted, monotonous, corrosive nightmare. And I would have really liked, with utmost sincerity, I would have liked to believe, as with any normal film, that this nightmare followed a plot development with a climax, an ending, and even an epilogue, but, from my observations, nothing of the sort takes place. Nothing goes anywhere. Nothing ever comes close to this supposedly ancient, time-tested, formulaic plotting.

"Now, wait a second. I can see by your face that you are nodding at me two-facedly, without believing a single word. In order to prove these facts to you to be clear as day and equally incontestable, I have decided to install myself at your place for a duration, not just overnight but to move in for a while so that I might live as closely as possible to your life, to feel the fiber of your assurance, your bluster, your readiness to force an entirely unfamiliar person—somebody who has done you no wrong—to pose questions to you as you leaned back sloppily in your chair, raised your gaze to the ceiling, and deigned to answer, as if this person had nothing left in life other than suffering the torture of constructing these questions, fine-tuning them one to the next, and then asking and waiting for each question to be crowned with an answer, like an action encountering with its opposite reaction, roots with a trunk, or fate with a character."

THOSE I MET

At roughly the center of the modest-sized area taken in by my astonished gaze—in the middle of a street fallen silent and drowning in autumnal fog—there dozed a person, over whom some concerned hand had thrown a plaid woolen blanket.

It is this person's pose that makes up an annotation to this book.

A NEEDLE IN A NIGHTSHIRT

Once upon a time there lived a woman who was kind, appealing, and pleasant in every respect. She is witty and wonderful, people said. There were others who simply praised her to the skies. She lived on Mala Zhytomyrska street in Kyiv, and she rejoiced every day when she went down the street, but not when she went up it. She was simplehearted to such an extent that she enjoyed walking downhill but not uphill. She was already about thirty years old, or maybe forty, or maybe twenty-five. Under the light of evening street lamps she was forty, but in the morning she looked almost like a child, especially if you saw her from the back, knowing full well she was buying milk at the supermarket.

What else is there to say? She was neat, attentive, and kind. Her best friend's children visited her on weekends, and she played with them while her friend ran around on dates. "I don't have any children yet," the woman used to say, "and I will make a gift of my love and care to these children."

Sometimes she would say remarkable things! Often she complained: "I am tired." And she pronounced these three words in her own special way, many times in a row. It was the same phrase we heard, almost the same intonation but, at the same time, we easily caught the difference in the sound of each word. The difference gave us pleasure. Us who? What is known for sure: We are not the sawdust lying under her bread box. Nor are we the three drops of blood that a neighbor left on the woman's doorstep.

But let us get back to her story. One evening the woman sat in her comfortable apartment over her usual housework and occupied herself with sewing. Some of her things long needed patching; it was time to reinforce a button on her light-weather coat. Anyway, what really happened was that, getting ready for bed, she took off her clothes, stood in front of the mirror, and sighed. For some time now she had dreamt of rounding out, putting on a little weight, but that evening she thought her ribs stuck out sideways like spokes in a broken wheel. When the woman saw the resemblance, she produced a protracted sound, *Oooooooo* … and immediately reached for a light roomy shirt, her favorite day-and nightshirt that swayed upon the varnished door of her wardrobe. She put it on and all of a sudden saw a small breach glinting by her breast, just off to the right. So then what do you think happened?

A woman like her would never leave even an insignificant perforation in her nightshirt unattended. She picked up an extremely fine silver needle, passed a refined white thread through the eye, and began to sew, stitch after stitch. Each stitch went through, obediently and smoothly, rejoicing at the woman's elegant snow-white fingers and tended, lilac nails.

You can probably guess what happened after. Everything was basically leading up to it. A gorgeous, perfect woman, with a snow-white face and snow-white arms, with a golden head of hair and a soft smile on her cherry lips, forgot the needle in her shirt. She carried out her design; she laid clean stitches across the puncture near her breast, but she put the needle literally out of her mind; she didn't even venture to cut off the thread. Rather, after the last stitch, she drove the needle through the shirt's thin fabric with a practiced gesture and simply left it in—right by her own heart, as it turns out.

A breathtaking story.

The horror of it.

We are dumbfounded but there's nothing we can do.

She might have cut the thread or at least hitched it around the needle or, for example, sealed the tip with wax, but no, nothing of the kind happened. The needle was forgotten in the shirt, seemingly forever. We emphasize—prior to the closure of the narrative—that the tear appeared by her heart and breast, somewhere on the left, but the woman had not yet been able to put on weight, fill out, "become rounder," as she had dreamt of being for many years, practically since childhood.

"I don't get it. She left the needle in—why did she do that? Because she could not feel it, yes? Or maybe there was a rupture in her body, where the needle easily found space? There are probably other explanations."

"There are no explanations. But the next story might make some things clearer."

THE WOMAN WHO CAUGHT
BABIES IN A MITT

I cannot remain silent about the following episode, which strikes me as at once flagrant and outrageous.

A woman's fate can really get around, especially if it's a woman of a certain age, who is shrill, insolent, and a witch. Nobody says you shouldn't believe in God. In God you should believe at least for the sake of your health, so as not to be sick your whole life, from when your teeth come in to when they fall out. But clever people believe in more than just God; they have a handle on even more complicated things or, how to better phrase it, wiser things. Take the elements for example. Do they not execute the orders of heavenly powers when somebody needs to be punished, given a tongue-lashing, or knocked about the jaw? Don't the elements love to torment us, taunt us, trample us down, spit in our faces? Well, if that's how it is, why not just start trusting them too?

Trust me, I'm a stranger to such superstitions and it's not me reasoning in this way but an entirely other woman, the one I'm about to talk about. I won't talk too much about her, though, as she asked me not to talk.

She was, you know, such a rare, amazing woman … and still is, living, flourishing, in Kyiv. Her profession was unusual but indispensable. What this woman did was deliver babies—naturally as an unregistered practitioner. She was, as I learned firsthand, magnificent at her job. Not one single social crisis could frighten her! Regardless of the political circumstances she was going like hotcakes. Strictly speaking, she serviced only several high-rises in the Kharkiv Development, and she did so in the following manner: she caught babies, babies in the process of being born, with a mitt. The mitt was huge. It was sewn from red and white cloth and made quite an impression.

As for the woman, she was big-boned, cheerful, on the late side of middle-age, and looked as if she'd turned sixty several centuries ago. She had a geometrically square face and three chiseled chins. Red and black birthmarks scattered over her cheeks, highlighting the daring of her quick, hazel eyes and the perkiness of her small, clear-cut nose. The flexibility of her crooked hands was frightening.

She was devoted to the Kharkiv Development, calling it "my ship," and had not left its limits for nearly fifty years. Every baby she helped to be born she recognized in the street, no matter the baby's age, even if they looked like an extremely old man. And every baby so recognized was ready to follow her call, obey her orders, and run after her to the end of the world, as if obeying powers far beyond those of a regular human being—something our statistics demonstrate fairly precisely. This, in fact, extremely dangerous woman of a certain age abused her position many times to purchase butter, milk, farmer's cheese, and other diabolical groceries that she consumed in their natural state or else used to prepare her magical dishes and medicines.

Why beat around the bush? That individual was a witch, and our entire neighborhood had been repeatedly subjected to unimaginable sufferings on account of her spite and whimsies. She effortlessly cursed whole buildings, which became the havens of evil powers and otherworldly phenomena. She sent mud rains onto courtyards; playgrounds rotted like overripe fruit fallen from trees.

Nobody in our neighborhood has ever met anyone more powerful than she. Never will anybody dare to doubt her or defy her will.

It is not impossible that all the information I impart to the astonished, note-taking woman is whispered to me by none other than her, from a distance, or that I have been living for a long time in total servitude to her iron will.

For this reason, I cannot help but set down:

You can't kill magic.

Witchcraft is forever.

Evil powers rule over the world.

I am resisting with all my strength; I am barely breathing; I am straining my breast, belly, hands; I am trying to erase these horrible words but I cannot. I simply cannot!

Sometimes we manage to sweep the yard, clean up the kitchen, go to work—and we think we have broken loose into freedom.

But no. The flowers in the courtyard have wilted; the flowerbeds have been ravaged by cars; the children are covered in dirt; the bushes refuse to bloom. There's an enormous mitt sticking out from the black hole of a window: Mariya Ilyinichna is getting ready for work.

MARCH 8: THE WOMAN
WHO COULD NOT WALK

This too can happen. In Kyiv on March 8, 2016, I happened to witness an astonishing spectacle: a woman lost the ability to walk in the course of an instant. They say this woman was in perfect health when she proficiently—with a quick, agile gait, almost an amble—reached the central street, Kreschatyk, relocated to the Maidan or Independence Square, and landed in the middle of a colorful holiday crush.

She strolled the square for a while; posed for a photograph with a monkey; bought beer at a kiosk and, in a show of benevolence, offered the gift of a beer to a stranger; ate ice cream; repeatedly glanced at the souvenir tables; comparison shopped without buying anything; eyed the clients of street cafés—and then, just like that, suddenly, without warning (no one saw it, there are no witnesses, we must take her at her word) she realized she could walk no further, performed a final, unprepossessing leap, and settled on a grey granite bench.

She sat there modestly, keeping her perfidious feet to herself. She didn't telephone anyone, didn't trouble her relatives and friends; she just faltered and quietly sat. She was waiting for things to take care of themselves. I walked up to her and we began discussing what happened to her, why she couldn't move from her seat, as if she had grown one with the bench and her feet had all but turned to stone.

The woman was categorically against any novel solutions and abrupt actions. She wished to sit on the bench a little, to ponder things, to turn things over this way and that, to wait it out, until she would finally realize what was happening to her. Only later, at some point in the future, after many hours, would she fall into a panic, scream, call her acquaintances one after another, demand to be saved, call the ambulance, and appeal to the mercy of passersby.

A *person* carried three bouquets past the woman and threw one of them to her. He threw the bouquet as if he were throwing a bone to a dog, not venturing a word. The woman caught the bouquet midflight and brought it to her face in a grand gesture, as if displaying her ability to inhale the smell of roses. Before we said goodbye, she found the time to tell me that today, on this one special day, *people* would turn their attention to women and try to do them favors. But, on other days, women were left to languish without attention in some backwater, with no holiday in the heart and no sense of personal dignity.

Then the woman smiled and confided to me that there is a certain secret she knows. Perhaps because of this secret she had lost the ability to walk and gradually became an inalienable part of the granite bench. "I am a living monument," the woman said jokingly, "but a monument that is soft, unstable, and wobbly; this is why, on such a day as today, I am really not worth your time." She maintained that events of historical importance, so to speak, could be taking place all around her, but she would remain sitting on the bench and every so often try to rise to her feet with a triumphant smile.

Cold and warm winds played with white and red rose petals while the woman examined, with undisguised interest, those who were rushing around her: the other women and *people*.

TWO WOMEN ON THE
AIRPLANE STAIRS: NO ONE MOVES
(MARCH 9, KYIV)

They were standing one step behind me.

The woman with long black hair, gentle face, large, quick eyes and a mercurial smile that warned no interlocutor in the world could hold her attention for more than a minute.

Her interlocutor wears a fur jacket that glitters in the sun; she is tall, with a serious gaze and an edifying tilt of the head.

WOMAN (*proudly*): He presented me with a large bouquet, full and fragrant—it's called "March Spring" in the catalogue. Managed to surprise me after all. That's what love means. My hands could hardly hold on to it as I was being photographed.

INTERLOCUTOR: They say it's a holiday invented by florists.

WOMAN: Still, it was quite a statement. My hands bled from the thorns, which is a proof of love.

INTERLOCUTOR: I definitely won't argue with that. But you know, love exists only when you have the power to love. A man I recently met told me how he lost all his powers, and then gained greater powers by far!

WOMAN (*absentmindedly*): He must have been a professional?

INTERLOCUTOR (*running with it*): He's one now. But he wasn't always. What a brave guy—one time he broke everything, almost every bone in his body: lower extremities, upper extremities, and his neck, too! He broke his pelvis and he broke his skull! He even broke his fingers and toes. Not by chance of course. He was jumping from somewhere because he was young and crazy, and maybe he crashed into something. I don't remember exactly.

The roar of aircraft engines muffles their voices, which then break through again.

WOMAN: People like him are given a special fate.

INTERLOCUTOR: You're telling me! For the longest time, nothing helped, not one doctor. He saw professors with international reputations; he went from clinic to clinic; he made for state medical institutes, but, even there, they just threw up their hands ... and, like, he couldn't even walk anymore! It was no laughing matter. He had no idea what to do. The pain was hellish, unbearable. It wouldn't let up day or night. He would stop by churches and pray, and then, one day, he just took off to China. He lost no time in China, he figured it out fast. First he found some celebrity acupuncturist. The treatment was a smashing success. He almost lost his mind with joy—the needles took the pain away.

WOMAN: Yes, I'd like to try acupuncture.

INTERLOCUTOR: But it was too soon to celebrate! In a month the pain returned, as often happens when it's cured just like that, without a spiritual practice. He was terrified, of course. He was in agony, nearly out of his mind. He tried this, he tried that. In the end he said, "To hell with Chinese medicine!" and bailed for Tibet. Naturally, somewhere in the distant, inaccessible mountains of Tibet he met a monk and moved in with him. The monk was absolutely inaccessible to anyone: secretive, antisocial, harsh, all about himself and his secret knowledge. But the man got lucky. The monk took him in and taught him a special breathing technique. If you practice this breath, it eases pain, health returns—but not just that, the mind empties as well. Of course it's not some simple art. You have to study it for years. So he spent several years in the monk's house and put his health back together, but then he got homesick and packed his bags. On the day of his leave-taking, the monk said to him: "You weren't given this knowledge just like that, but for a larger purpose. You can help other people. Go from spa-salon to spa-salon and teach the art that I taught you—save lives!" And, would you believe it, he took on the task. He obeyed the monk!

INTERLOCUTOR: Is he one of us?

INTERLOCUTOR: The man is Ukrainian. We met at a spa-weekend in the Maldives. He was the consultant for our group.

WOMAN: I wouldn't have thought one of us could do it.

INTERLOCUTOR: The owners of the spa are themselves initiates. They don't just live like everybody; they live in a special way. They've gradually transitioned into another category of people: into people of a new quality. You know, there are people who are very well-off: They have so much money that they think of wealth differently than we do. They look at money with a fresh gaze, and, practically swimming in money, they despise it, or they love it not with our love but with a more perfect love—and this is how they move on to another stage of development!

WOMAN: Like stars?

INTERLOCUTOR: Close but sometimes even more so. Having no wants, they are saving our planet, the so-called lesser creatures and others. So these two initiates bought a chain of spa-salons on different islands and from there they announced the Epoch of the Struggle for a New World. Initially we were all simply astounded by what we heard and saw. They even permitted the consultant and his smarmy Italian friend to come to us for breakfast. They sat him down at the same table with us! He was working in the sauna, teaching us the breath, and sometimes even dined with us! Dinners were also very instructive. To such an extent that I am still being instructed, from memory. Even now, as I am speaking with you, my learning process continues automatically—it flows somewhere inside the spinal cord and just keeps going.

WOMAN: I tell you, we have so far to go to reach that level of understanding. But the time to start moving toward it is now. Enough procrastinating! We are behind everyone else, at the tail end. Ukraine has never yet hosted interventions at this level—how long do we still have to wait?

The noise of aircraft engines rises. Our turn has come. Everyone who stood on the stairs enters the cabin and takes their seats. The two young women settle into first class and I do not hear the rest of their conversation.

THE WOMAN WHO
FELL SICK

Once in Kyiv there lived and worked, by the sweat of her brow, a certain woman who at last became indisposed. She lived entirely alone in a residential district that many called the Lap, the UFO, or the Epic Fail. It is worth noting that this woman had not fallen sick for four months in a row; yet she was not somebody known for her ruddy constitution and had been sick constantly, even continuously, before her stretch of good health.

Cold winter months passed by. The heating hardly warmed the room, which was also damp all the time from articles of laundry drying over the stove like large-winged bats. Still—for four months already, if you start with November, this woman was as healthy as a barn mouse. And it was March outside, after all.

No common cold, no runny nose, no sore throat—the poor woman was simply bursting with health, so much so that she no longer felt human, although she was holding down three jobs. She felt like an unfeeling mechanism, a clock with a human face, a primitive piece of software, or a cell-phone smiley.

And all because she stopped getting sick. How it made her suffer!

"What if I stopped eating," she thought to herself, "would I keep on living as if nothing had happened? Before, I would sleep for four hours a night and it was never enough and so I'd get sick. But now I sleep the same four hours and I'm totally healthy!

"I used to lie in bed, exhausted with a high temperature, and count the electric cables outside the window. Now I sometimes forget my house even has windows!

"Lord, you have punished me with health! What have I done to deserve this? Was it that time I unwittingly took someone else's merit pay and did not return it?

"Or maybe it was that time I was buying potatoes and received more change than I was supposed to, and I said nothing to the saleswoman but simply took the money and bought candy with it?

"Is there no justice, is there no mercy that the Lord has for his servant Martha?"

"Ha-ha, Martha! You're no Martha!" (A voice suddenly rang out above her head.)

This digression might veer beyond the bounds of my study, but I fail to understand what this woman could have expected if she even lied about her own name during prayer? Could it be that *someone* would stir so much as a finger over such trifles, over such petty and stupid, if you allow me to say so, requests?

What a naive piece of reasoning! It's high time you know that grace may descend on people as insignificant as her.

Because, after a brief pause, she heard the same voice again. It flew down straight from the sky, sharp and clear at the same time.

"Be of good comfort," it said. "You shall no longer have health, Malvina. For your prayer has been answered, and you shall be struck down by illness, and that illness shall be the common cold."

"Thank you, O Lord! Have mercy!" cried out the happy Malvina (for that was indeed her name, I can vouch for it), and she ran home as fast as she could. When she arrived she headed straight for the kitchen, which also served as the coziest of bedrooms. She took off her jacket, hung her sodden jeans on the radiator, put on a sweater, tied a scarf around her throat, and lay down in bed.

A miracle! That was the very moment the courteous and considerate illness was waiting for. A common cold accompanied by a mild sore throat, without any complications: it came to Malvina only after she settled snugly beneath the three plain blankets that served as her duvet.

Days and nights passed. After that incident, Malvina found an additional job, her fourth one—at a church. There, for no pay whatsoever, she cleaned, washed, laundered, comforted the afflicted, and aided the parishioners any way she could. She sewed, baked communion bread and cookies, prepared jam, poured monastic wine into bottles, carried in the wine, carried out boxes, made presents of head kerchiefs to parishioners, distributed five winter hats, tended to the war-wounded, as well as to a dying woman, and fulfilled a great many other useful and important tasks.

With these holy sacrifices the wonderful woman strove to thank her new best friend—the one who so constantly and loyally took care of her from then on, the one who was all-powerful and magnificent, unique and elegant, practical and energetic, generous and optimistic, faultless and organized, courageous and modest, majestic and always positive—the owner of a gorgeous voice that rang out as if from nowhere ... of course you know who I'm talking about.

THE FLORIST

The florist is a woman who loves flowers. As for me, I confess I had been in love with the florist for several months in a row. She has a better grasp of flowers than anybody else. The words *ranunculus* and *hellebore* cannot astonish her. But she very much likes to be astonished—to gasp and innocently turn her daisy of a face toward her interlocutor; to open her eyes wide, grasp the back of a chair with a fluttering hand, and set her mouth into an O.

Actually, she also took after flowers by being imperturbable; her rare beauty, too, she got from flowers. Each morning she raised the shutters of her store, neared the window, and smiled, pausing for some moments in the prospect of aspidistra and bupleurum.

Practically no one ever noticed her astonishingly well-assembled face. I've never seen a single passerby stop to admire her. In the afternoon, right after lunch break, she would stand for some time, leaning against the plastic window frame, as indifferent pedestrians continued on their way; only rarely did anyone enter her flower shop. I liked to stop by and study how she gathered bouquets, arranged flowers and branches in vases, cut stems, tore off leaves. The florist was familiar with exotic, barely existent words that denoted hues, tints, petals. She pronounced them clearly and with joy, the way a child recites for the first time a poem learned by heart: *Bring them closer to the light, those Persian buttercups the color of ivory.* She was convinced that her customers bought not so much flowers as the names of flowers.

This acquaintance of mine lived in Donetsk and loved more than anything in the world to make up designations for flower arrangements, bouquets, and flower baskets. One winter morning I found her glowing and happy behind the counter. Her brightly painted lips, perfectly positioned in the lower half of her mother-of-pearl face, triumphantly announced: "Listen to the new names, now chosen! Attend to their melodic form but do not ignore their philosophical significance:

Breakfast in Venice
Spring Pageantry Wow
*Absolute Spring**

A Roman Bedchamber
An Ukrainian Mystery
March Spring."

---

* Original in English.

She waited for my approval, which was swiftly granted. She had invented the bouquet names for the next season— spring—and she counted on its rapid approach.

The florist was a successful, practical woman, with an excellent understanding not only of flowers but also of bookkeeping. At the same time, she was entirely unsuited for real life. As she herself frequently told me, it was only inside her store—which at some point had transformed into the meaning of her life—that she knew how to exist. She decided to abolish weekends even, and in the winter of 2014 she worked on Saturdays and Sundays.

What is this story I am telling really about? Does it make any sense to continue? In fact, the story doesn't exist, the narrative doesn't continue, it breaks off. The florist disappeared. The house where she lived was destroyed. Her store was refitted into a warehouse of propaganda materials. Her regular customers left Donetsk long ago.

Recently and purely by accident I bumped into one of the people who had often bought flowers from her, and he confessed to having heard something about the florist. He said that she went off into the fields and joined the partisans. That's exactly what he said: "Went off into the fields." But on what side her partisan unit was fighting and where those fields were, he had no idea. The florist, he reminded me, never had a nose for politics. She was a flowerworm of sorts; she even classified people into differ- ent kinds of flowers. She had never occupied herself with anything in life other than flowers, he lamented.

"She must be fighting on the side of the hyacinths," he suddenly declared, and broke into laughter. We fell silent as he stared at me and waited for me to give his sense of humor its due. "Time is passing, I'm growing smarter; I am beginning to understand which way the wind is blowing and where we're heading," he added. "I am not the person I was. You can't fo. ! me at one try! Kyiv has taught me a thing or two. This isn't our naive Donetsk. But I still have my sense of humor; I don't have to sift through my pockets for it." And again he broke into laughter and then walked off with a triumphant gait, following his own business.

THE MANICURIST

A certain young woman, almost an adolescent, lived completely alone in Anthracite, in a large, two-room, forty-eight-square-meter apartment. To her the apartment had neither borders nor limits. She spent much of her time at home, and rushed to return there right after getting off work. She was a manicurist. She had no friends, or almost no friends, and her parents lived far away, in another country. She lived, in other words, independently, in an apartment that she had inherited and considered a palace. Every morning she went outside to do a bit of shopping, take a walk on the familiar concrete paving squares, evaluate the situation in town and, if all was well, go to work.

When she left her home she would never walk in the direction of the city center, for the city center made her mildly—or else wildly—apprehensive. She only took the familiar route, from the apartment to the grocery store; next to the grocery store stood the manicure salon, which did not belong to her. But the owner of the salon had recently found herself in another country. This is why the manicurist had a little key that she used to open the door to someone else's salon, and there she would heroically work for ten or twelve hours sometimes, reporting to nobody, not giving much thought to security, since she carried home the expensive, sparkling clean manicure equipment each day. She had side-swept bangs, a complexion that was always fresh, nails filed in the most meticulous manner—and on the nails of her index and little fingers she would paint arabesques. Some thought this skill of hers an artistic gift. Others who noticed her started to fantasize about becoming close to her, or at least better acquainted.

Come to think of it, she must have had friends after all, just not in our city. It's not really possible for such a pretty, personable, athletic young woman to have no friends.

We loved her very much. We didn't understand that she was alone and had nobody to help her. Nor did we immediately notice that the salon was gone, and that a supplies warehouse had appeared in its place. We knew for certain that she hadn't left the city. Everyone on the street was sure that she hadn't run off anywhere, or moved away. There was compelling evidence to the contrary.

When we were finally brave enough to address the stranger working in the former salon, when we finally dared to ask about her whereabouts and situation, he answered more or less as follows: "She came down with a cold. Don't ask stupid questions—she came down with a cold, an illness that makes being a manicurist impossible, because it makes your hands tremble. For reasons of safety and hygiene, we gave her temporary leave. But don't worry about it; she'll soon feel better and call you, if you are her regular clients, or she'll again open up her salon right here...."

We've been waiting for her return for a long time now. It's been more than two years and I'm still waiting for her.

MY SISTER

I saw her standing, scanning the rows of cars.

July 5, 2014. Strelkov's forces were leaving Slavyansk. A grey, smoky day at the end of many drawn-out months. Dull flashes of headlights, wind, and the din of car horns. The fighters must have been waiting for someone to arrive so that they could move out.

Broken windowpanes on the ground floor of a neighboring high-rise, black puddles after rain, shouts, roll call—but she was standing firm.

I felt a momentary silence descend on everything. The pedestrians were all gone, as if they had died out. The silence had seized not just the nearby streets, where solitary cars stood with passengers ready to depart, but the entire city. Rows of windows were lit; electrical wires dangled like snakes from some of the open window frames to suck the electricity out of neighboring apartments.

Cars, soiled and sullen, were collecting little by little at the city center.

There she was, still standing at the intersection, apparently trying to speak to someone in one of the vehicles.

"I'm not coming with you!" she suddenly shouted, her voice rising above the car horns. "I'm staying here! I decided not to go!"

My sister has decided. Only a minute ago she seemed set on the contrary. All the days that these people, such strangers to us, lived in our city, she cooked for them, offered them support, listened in on their conversations, and then proudly told us of their military plans, how they would capture the Kharkiv Region and—slowly but surely—Kyiv. But now she has announced that she was staying. Staying where? Could it be with us, who had become strangers to her over the last few weeks?

On the other hand, her life—her desires, dreams, and hopes—made sense only so long as our city was occupied by armed men, soldiers, unknowns. It felt like ages ago that she had shared her dream with us of uniting her life with the life of one of the strangers, and there had already been talk of the wedding.

And then, without warning, two broad-shouldered guys jumped out of a vehicle. They appeared beside her as fast as lightning and a moment later she disappeared behind the slammed door of the car.

I forbade myself to understand anything or think about anything.

None of us had the courage to come closer, if only to find out where they were taking her and when we might see her again.

We lost all communication with her. We silenced ourselves and never spoke of her. It's hard to believe it but weeks passed and we lived on without knowing anything. Where could we go for information? Who could we call? However it may be, we never bothered to find out where she ended up.

She reappeared several months later. There's nothing more to tell. She doesn't complain; she lives with us; she goes to work as before. At work they didn't count her absence against her. Which is to say that they paid her salary for the time she was gone. It's the one thing we managed to do for her. And it's no small thing, no small thing by our standards. She doesn't tell us anything, but we don't ask her anything either.

NEIGHBOR HISTORIES

"Of course the threshold separating life from death has long been called the Threshold of Laughter.

Whereas the wall separating the bedroom from the kitchen went by the name of Penny Pitch. And the lamp hanging over the bed, Cocaine.

I think up names for everything I hold dear. Even the mouse in our apartment I used to call Lucy until she got nailed. You can name anything anything: everybody knows that. And I can recall several names if I allow myself to, and I may even make a few up—as so much has vanished into thin air, gone up in smoke, drifted downriver without a paddle, or fallen off the face of the earth."

Such were the thoughts of a certain woman who in the recent past ran a large department in a major company, but today washes the office floor of a notary public in Kyiv. In winter, she went out for bread in a mink or marten coat, but now she comes to work in a down jacket that she feels is her shame and her curse.

And it's all because the woman's spacious, fairly recently renovated and refurnished home fully moved into her consciousness after it was destroyed. The home's new existence inside her mind supposedly prevented her from settling into a new life.

She moved to Kyiv—"pulled my skin out of the fire," as she liked to say—and "selflessly threw myself at work, whatever work there was to be had."

They hired her at a small, private notarial practice that merely seemed private. The woman knew very well that everything private in her country was only partially private. So she was not surprised to learn that she was offered a cleaning-staff salary fit for a public hospital rather than a respectable institution.

On that day and hour, when the bell rang, when the pathetic sum of the salary was announced, a woman like her—educated, pushy, lonely, willful, a little angry— should have bolted, fleeing as far as her feet would carry her, or done anything, anything except stay in the accursed office with minuscule cubicles and walls that narrowed toward the ceiling.

How difficult could it have been for a woman with her connections and reputation to make a few proper phone calls and set her life straight? If only she had made the slightest effort, she certainly could have found her place under the sun and made a nest for herself—a nest no worse than what others made. But when she learned one blood-curdling detail after another about her new employment—like, around here the cleaning staff buy mops and rags at their own expense, and also the rest of the material—her resolve to correct her circumstances miraculously broke, over and over, like waves, against the apparition of a detailed plan of her former home, the rooms and old vaults and basement spaces that were in need of structural repairs, which the whole cooperative had been pushing for.

It so happened that everyone who lived in her part of the building was well-to-do, successful, and established in life. One worked as the director of a housing management office; another was a deputy director of technology; there was a capital construction project manager and also a branch director of a bank. She did not feel particularly disposed toward any of them, or rather, she thought they weren't fit to tie her shoes. Now she spent entire days racking her brains over where they had disappeared to and what fate had befallen them.

They say that one public relations manager—from the second floor—went off to live in the countryside, where he grows potato varieties never seen before in the region, like a red potato in the shape of a heart called the VIP Tuber.

One very well-known and affluent woman, whose profession I will not share with you, became an architect, they say, in the neighboring city. But this is difficult to verify—one must simply accept it.

The bank branch director has taken up stalking, or rather, he became what they call a stalker: someone who guides visitors from out of town around destroyed buildings and shows them holes the size of a cannonball. He is the only one who takes pride in his profession and, when the conversation gets arounds to political controversies, he repeats that whatever happens must be for the best.

What befell all the others? How do they support themselves now? How do you get from the toilet to the kitchen without stepping into what once was my apartment hallway? How can you avoid the bathroom on your way to the living room?

Where does the corridor end and the bedroom begin?

These questions agitated the woman to such an extent that sometimes, as she was washing the floor, she would suddenly utter miscellaneous answers loud and clear, throwing her washrag into the pail with such force that droplets flew at the clients, which did not facilitate the delivery of speedy solutions for their legal quandaries.

The employer wanted to fire the woman, but instead suggested she work at night rather than during the day. She kept her position. The last I heard she continues to come in at midnight and finishes cleaning around six in the morning. So you mustn't let evil tongues claim that it's difficult for our refugees to find work in the big city.

A WOMAN FINDS A JOB

One young and very capable woman set her heart on finding a job in Kyiv. In fact, she was at the end of her rope and hanging by a thread. She lived in a small rental, and her savings were running out. Moreover, for her whole life she had dreamt of making a substantial contribution to what people call arts and culture. Also, from her early years she knew that she was intelligent and blessed with almost all of the talents proper to the human race: she sang, danced, composed music and poetry, and could depict flowers with watercolors like nobody's business. Not only that, but she had also received a university degree in economics, and knew her way around the code of law.

For some reason, no suitable position had popped up in weeks and yet there were bills due and due ... too bad for you, my precious weeks! The approach of that day when she had to pay her next month's rent filled her with dread;

she was losing weight and sometimes, in the evenings, she would peek into a future so bleak that it frightened her, causing her to flee to a café or anywhere else so as not to be alone. Nearby, on Prorizna Street, she squandered the remains of her fortune on a small cup of gourmet coffee. As everyone knows, coffee in Kyiv sometimes costs an arm and a leg and, in a certain sense, serves to compensate those who carelessly throw away their worldly goods for their mental anguish.

So when she came across the announcement below, she immediately telephoned, arranged for an interview, and found herself a job. Since then, she hasn't picked up the phone or returned my calls.

THE NATIONAL ACADEMY
OF ARTS OF UKRAINE
IS LOOKING FOR AN ADMINISTRATOR.

If you are a young and goal-oriented woman between 18 and 25 years of age, with a model's good looks, friendly facial features, top communication and computing skills, and a commitment to personal growth, you may apply for the position of administrator at the Academy, with responsibilities that include managing the President's correspondence and accompanying him on business-related travel. Salary: 4,000 UAH, negotiable.

THE WOMAN WITH THE BLACK, BROKEN UMBRELLA

March 2016, Kyiv

I don't want to write about her; I have no wish to recall her. She forgot her umbrella at the bus stop—believe me, there's no need to recall that incident—then she was making her way to the bus stop in the pouring rain to retrieve it—if I remember correctly—and then, when she finally took it into her hands, couldn't manage to open it.

Apparently it was her last umbrella.

Can anything be more affecting than events of this sort? Lacking an umbrella, striving to possess it, a fluttering hand extending in its direction. Perhaps only the need to think and speak of such insignificant, trivial things.

A man's umbrella, medium-sized, semiautomatic. A black inkblot.

The bus stop: a transparent cage. She was making her way to that spot of black in the rain, stealing toward it, and in the meantime, as she communicated to me afterward, remembered a recent incident, not long ago, in another city, when she was making her way to retrieve a black rag under fire. She recalled her tremors, her stupidity. This woman moved to Kyiv from a region where the war raged—but here, against any common sense, she continued with her wartime habits, her wartime tricks of desperate relations with objects, things, the streets.

I didn't want to talk about her; it's painful for me to recall her face, sharply cut by thin rifts of wrinkles. She said the same things too often. But lately I've been doing that too. She made overly insistent attempts to explain her despair to me; she wanted even more—for me to put a high value on the pain, anxiety, and fear that do not let her rest.

I will never manage to shed light on that clinging *bewilderment,* the distractedness that does not let go. I can only try to reproduce it, to list its existential forms: the sudden lurch from the house to the bus stop for the umbrella; the fit of wrestling with it; the engagement that launches away a coat button, recently bought and resewn, while the spokes bare themselves and poke out, casting shadows across the face. The umbrella will not open. It is abandoned out of wrath on the bus stop bench as the abandoner rushes to the closest café for a breather. Although it's not really a café but an unprepossessing kiosk on the Boulevard of International Friendship. Here they offer bad coffee for 8 hryvni, and for 6 a glass of tea. Our eyes meet each other. She commences her eternal lament; she sings her sorrows to the kiosk woman. The kiosk woman looks at her with envy, for she is a free woman whom the rapacious and venal kiosk owner doesn't hold between her claws.

The kiosk woman says, "These blocks of butter here have almost melted. I would have liked to butter myself, I would have smeared the butter all over me, I wouldn't have spared even my hair, because in this kiosk your skin turns to tin. I both live and sleep here, I'm cooped up here the whole week. Only sometimes for a half hour I dash off to the house next door—to brush my teeth, wash my face—otherwise I'm here, there's no going outside, like a bunny in a terrarium."

Both women are anxious. Neither knows what to do with herself. As for me it is by chance that I happen to be near them, and we succeed in holding a conversation for some pitiful fifteen minutes.

And the woman who had been making her way toward her umbrella, who has just now caught her breath, again wants to take off from where she is, to run through snow and ice to the bus stop for her umbrella, which she abandoned in the middle of an iron bench where it lies like a black stain, like a crushed tube of paint, or a nebulous ink spill. She left it there at the bus stop though the umbrella had allegedly gone through unbelievable hardships with her—the things that umbrella had seen over the past year, what hadn't it lived through.

The kiosk woman tries to hold her back, appealing to her common sense, reason, dignity, honor, and pride, and to her not having finished her coffee.

The woman throws us a cunning look in which I see pity and disdain, and says that in any case she must buy some milk near the Lybidska metro and she will now proceed in that direction, past the bus stop, naturally.

She tears herself from us. Quickly, stumbling and jumping

over small obstacles, as if dashing for the next shelter, she careens to the bus stop, takes the umbrella into her hands, and attempts to open it. We've seen it all before! Pointless.

But now she doesn't throw the umbrella back on the bench; she takes it into her hands and starts walking aslant, in the direction of a small park, and I follow behind her for some reason, gradually nearing her.

I hear what she says to her umbrella: "You black scab. What did I buy you for. You always go about dirty, sick, infected. You can never be by yourself. You're all gnawed up by illnesses and infections, you're a scab, and I'm going to get rid of you, believe you me. I won't act like I'm sorry for you anymore. I carried you into the park yesterday, I left you on a bench by the trash bins, but you laid out your terms, you bastard, you abortion, you waited me out. But today I'll carry you into such wilderness that lying around will get you nowhere, you'll be lying around for nothing, you thankless wretch. When I asked you to be like everyone else, to do what you're told, you just had to have it your way, you wretch, you. When I was cleaning, washing everything around me which means you also— it was like zero fudge, you just went on being yourself. That's what you care about. To be yourself! But I can't do this anymore! I'm at the end of my rope! I forgot the last time I was myself! I'm exhausted! I'm sick and tired of tending to you everywhere, sick and tired of coming to your rescue. So you just stay where you are, friend, I'm going off to the Lybidska station. Believe me, it'll be easier that way for you and for me."

She disappeared behind one of the buildings. I did not follow her any longer.

THE SEER OF DREAMS

She had many talents and even more gifts. She lived in a small village in the neighborhood of Poltava, then in Sumy, and then in Kyiv—in second homes that belonged not to friends but to people she barely knew. She had one tracksuit, black, with a velvet trim, of a fairly distinguished cut. She also owned a jacket, loafers, boots, a purse, a makeup bag, and a few other things—basically, she traveled light.

She wanted to meet people, find a best friend, and get a job. She could've become close friends with somebody, no doubt: she was a person you could trust. She didn't want to think about bad, nasty, sad, heavy, and depressing things anymore, or maybe she never did think about such things. Why be gloomy, when, after a row of the dreariest of days, a bright sunny day may follow? Even if it's minus seven degrees outside and the snow shows no intention of melting under the sun.

She moved to Kyiv in the fall of 2015. She spent the winter alone, in a cold, empty country cottage located on a dead-end offshoot of one of the inconspicuous streets in Rusanivka Gardens.

Six weeks ago snowdrifts surrounded her cozy-seeming little brick house. For some reason it was on her street that no one thought to clean up the snow. Cars couldn't move. At night, loud noises came from one of the other houses, the one with a dubious reputation. Visitors had arrived before the snowstorm and decided to stay put. They turned night into day, inverting their sleep, though every so often one of them woke up and wandered outside, possibly to perform something very night-like in the daylight. Then—from late in the evening until morning—screams, screeches, the sounds of breaking dishes and of somebody weeping all issued forth through the fogged-up window panes.

A day finally came, or rather a morning, when someone knocked on the woman's window. She answered the door and saw in front of her an attractive, totally drunk young woman, a neighbor. The neighbor wore a skirt; she had a red-and-white scarf dashingly tied around her in place of a blouse and jacket, and there were pine branches attached to her hair. The red scarf and the branches made her look like a wounded doe. Her hands and shoulders were bare but she didn't seem to be cold at all.

"Moo-oo-oo," said the neighbor, and made to ask the woman a question but failed and mooed once again.

Our woman immediately invited her in for a cup of hot tea. The neighbor stepped, almost naked, into somebody else's cold house. This was the beginning of their beautiful friendship.

They spent the whole evening together and had a fabulous time, just the two of them. They laughed, played cards, and baked apples. They went to the neighbor woman's house to throw snow and beer-bottle caps at the visitors, and then the two of them came back and made coffee with brandy.

Then the neighbor returned home—not for long, just for a half-hour—and our woman fell asleep.

She had a dream. She dreamt that she was alone, sledding down a huge hill in a wild wood inhabited by bears who were speaking in various foreign languages. One of the bears picked up her sled and tossed it to another bear. And the next bear did the same. She was flying in her sled between one pair of paws and another, and it felt fun and marvelous. Laughing uproariously, she made to hug the bears, but they bared their teeth and joked like English lords. Then she dreamt that a huge castle appeared in the middle of the forest, somewhat like the dacha of a certain major official from Sumy. She entered the castle, and in the great hall she saw a broad table, and on that table lay a live, good-natured fish who called her over with its tail. She approached the fish but then recognized the high official, Valery Nikolaevich, at the very top of a long staircase. He stood towering above, a heavy gold crown pressed down on his forehead. The castle was enchanted. A dragon kidnapped prince Valery Nikolaevich and aged him to his sixtieth year. A giant bird flew up from under the ceiling and grasped the woman to carry her away from this accursed place.

At that point the woman woke up.

Then she fell asleep again.

And she dreamt yet another dream. She dreamt that she was walking in Kyiv, on Saint Sophia Street, heading uphill from Independence Square. The old trees swept the road before her with their leaves. Prehistoric animals roamed around—dinosaurs, pterodactyls, and among them elephants in saddles adorned with traditional embroidery. Suddenly she saw the first Ukrainians, who looked hardly different from the Ukrainians of the present day. They were kind, and also naive, and also a bit sly. She was walking up Saint Sophia Street and then turned right and saw a house with fabulous balconies. On one of the balconies were vats filled with magnificent flowers. On this balcony appeared a gorgeous woman who looked like her neighbor; she held an emerald watering can in her hands, and she started to water the flowers. At this moment the dreamer felt a great thirst and awoke again.

So what do you think happened next? She saw the neighbor woman standing over her, and behind the neighbor stood several of the neighbor's friends. How fantastic! They all came to visit her, gathering in her cold house! She was no longer alone in her cottage!

She treated her visitors to tea and told them about her first dream, and then her second.

The visitors were stunned. One of them, whose neck was blue with stubble, roared, "You didn't dream those dreams! You made them all up, you sheep! Nobody dreams dreams like that!"

Another man, who looked like an educated person, declared, "Even geniuses don't receive dreams like that!" He, too, couldn't believe the woman.

But the woman responded with a trill of innocent laughter, and replied, "Neighbors, what's with you? Why would I make up my dreams? Do I have nothing else to do except invent castles and forest, birds and elephants, and prehistoric animals, too! Why should I waste time with such nonsense?"

The company took note of her argument and decided to stop accusing the woman of such disgraceful chicanery as the idle invention of dreams.

Indeed, the woman dreamt all the time! And these dreams completely transformed her life.

The neighbor woman, who became her best friend, opened a coffeehouse in the center of Kyiv and gave our woman a job there, where she served coffee called "Delicious Dream," "Meditation," "Magical Worlds," and "Flying Over an Ocean of Wishes."

The little coffeehouse grew more and more successful day after day.

The dreamer's father fell gravely ill, and she started to send him money regularly. The new best friend, regarding the dreamer with great favor, had her father checked into such a prestigious hospital that, out of happiness, he altogether stopped calling his daughter. He was afraid of jinxing his luck, as he later explained.

At the coffeehouse where the woman worked no one discussed terrible, heavy, or frightening things. Politics was forbidden. To this day you still can't discuss anything sad, depressing, hopeless, or frightening there.

A tested company of friends meets at the coffeehouse every Friday to listen to the two or three or even five most recent dreams dreamt by the waitress.

Here is another one of her dreams, with her own commentary:

"I dreamt that we bought multicolored wafer straws for hot chocolate. They were beautiful and unusual. If you brought one up to your mouth, a melody would pour out of the wafer, a melody so beautiful that all who heard it wanted to cry and laugh at the same time. And people on Independence Square in Kyiv were crying and laughing when they heard the music coming out of our coffeehouse. Some of them started to dance. Oh! How happy I was to hear this gorgeous music! It was magical and divine! Because of it, the neighboring lanes filled with musicians and actors dressed up as different animals. The actors danced and then began to eat the musicians, but the musicians were not in pain: They enjoyed it! A steaming rivulet of their blood ran into our coffeehouse and I threw myself toward it, got down on all fours and drank. And at that very moment I felt that I was turning into a completely different person—a European, an inhabitant of a great and ancient land. I turned into an inhabitant of a country that knows neither frontiers nor obstacles, neither variety in manner of dress nor that in ways of professing love.

"I used to be an ordinary girl but then everything changed so irrevocably!

"My dreams have made me successful; my dreams tell a future that is not only mine—they tell the fate of the whole world, especially that of Ukraine and Europe.

"Yesterday I dreamt of a gorgeous dog—a red hunting hound. She had two necks and two heads. She ran southwest in front of me, opening up a passage toward

the lowlands of the Podil quarter of Kyiv. She was courageous; she prophesied happiness for all of us, saying that
we will soon attain prosperity—this year, or next year at
the latest."

THE LONELY WOMAN

Fate delivered her to Kyiv. She didn't know what to do about it. She came from Donetsk, where she had lived her whole life in her parents' small, one-family house. She had enough in her purse. That's what they say, "in her purse," although her actual purse was empty, full of wind. The wind part, really, is a hyperbole. She simply possessed something to her name, that's it. That's how they say it around here, "to her name," although her name had nothing to do with it; she was not a name brand. In short, she had some inviolable reserves that she had to unseal and start systematically spending.

What a fascinating woman! So said an alcoholic of a certain age from the Vernissage Café in Podil, in reference to Sveta Orletz, and immediately shifted his attention to some entirely different object. Tenderly he studied a chair decorated with painted crucifixions. Again they couldn't control themselves, those Kyivan Orthodox Christian thugs: Jesuses and crosses, scratched on with a childish but, at the same time, none too sober hand, also covered the broad wooden table. The man made the sign of the cross and piously bowed to the chair. Sveta produced a sob. She was sitting right next to me, still lonely as hell. Or rather, she was so lonely she was "headed for hell," as she put it, "in a handbasket."

She doesn't know what to do in Kyiv. She's at a total loss. "There's nowhere to start living here. There's not even a branch to catch onto, or a stair to put your foot on. No points of support. Maybe these points are hidden from me alone? They're scattered all over the place like glitter around a bandshell, and I am the only person who doesn't see them. Points of support in Kyiv are like the will-o'-the-wisp. It's really easy here to fall into viscous swamp mud and sink lower and lower. I'll start to scream—'Help! Help!'—and the only thing that might happen is some old goat would look my way to feast his eyes on the last moments of my life!

"Here I am sitting next to you, you look kind, inquisitive, but I feel bored with you, too, I know we'll never become best friends."

That's me she's talking about.

Every time Sveta Orletz found herself next to someone in Kyiv—at the same table, on the same bench—she felt the most profound disappointment. No one could comfort her or calm her down. The proximity of a human creature aroused in her an even more tragic sense of life than total solitude. She had not one person she could talk to, and often repeated to herself, "Not one?! No one around! Good God, are these even people? They are like soup leftovers, not people. They mumble, they swallow words, you can't make out what they're carrying on about. They go wide-eyed and goggle at you, but as for some clear, heartfelt exchange, no chance. I'm dying being around them like a bush with no water, like a fireplace with no fire, like a freshly stolen car in the hands of bandits. I'm dying, and I have no one to turn to in the end and say, 'You were gracious to me!' Honestly, I would like to give my life to someone—but I haven't a single candidate whatsoever! Maybe we're all part of a lost generation?"

At these musings my meeting with Svetlana came to an end.

I saw her again after several weeks. Sveta was rescued by a certain Kyivan contrivance. She was rescued by a security policeman's mirrored booth, or, more specifically, by the booth installed on Volodymyrska Street, near building number 16.

One day, during a morning hour, Sveta was walking on Volodymyrska—in despair, of course, as well as in some terror of the extent to which a person can feel rejected, miserable, and at loose ends. She wasn't in a hurry; she was walking slowly, and, as it had lately become a habit with her, she pulled faces, stuck out her tongue, bulged her eyes, puffed her cheeks, raised her shoulders, smiled wildly, and squinted. Sveta was screwing up her visage, making a mean mien, or, as she used to say, outing herself. She had apparently run out of all other suitable means for finding inner balance.

But then, completely unexpectedly for her, with no portent or premonition, as if in a fairy tale, the doors of the booth that Sveta was passing opened, and a policeman's long torso angled across the threshold. His simple smile whispered a few words of encouragement and enticement. She had nothing to lose. Sveta immediately popped into the booth and found herself alone with an entirely unknown person in a fairly small contained space, where only one of them could sit in a chair, while the other had to make do with a narrow rug, spread out almost entirely beneath the chair.

The two of them certainly had a lot in common. They suddenly found each other, and spent every day together since then. Moreover, as of that day, abrupt and unforeseen changes for the better started to take shape in their lives, as often happens with those on whom happiness falls out of thin air.

LENA IN DANGER

All this took place in the two-thousands, at the end of a long historical epoch. Nobody was surprised any longer. It was all elementary, simple. Because that's the kind of country we have, okay? The unprotected kind.

You can't really live in this country—you're threatened from every side at every moment. That's the kind of country it is. If you had the luck to be born here, you take things as they come.

I was just over fifteen when Papa started explaining to me how dangerous it is to live here, in our country. I didn't know anything yet.

Ten years later I called him from Leipzig. I was having a hard time adjusting; I missed him. I wanted to see him and the whole family, I wanted to go for a walk with my brother, to run into chance acquaintances.

But my father said to me, "Better you stay where you are." His voice was made of iron.

"That's the kind of country we have." This is how dangerous—unbelievably dangerous—it got to be to live in our country.

It made me uneasy. I felt as if I heard Papa admit it for the first time. "You know, daughter, it's become so dangerous to live in our country." But I laughed to myself: When wasn't it dangerous to live in our country?

It was actually horrible, brutal to hear those words at that moment. Because when you hear such words you really do feel the danger.

That's the kind of country we have!

I never walked the streets as freely in Ukraine as in Weimar or Leipzig. Although here you don't feel entirely safe now either. When my friend was walking home recently, a man followed, caught up with her, and simply punched her in the face. He hit her as hard as he could, he didn't spare any effort. Nothing like this has ever happened to any of my friends in Germany before.

What was she guilty of? She was simply walking home, singing a little tune—she likes to sing. It wasn't late yet; our neighborhood is peaceful. As he walked past her, he punched her in the face. Just like that! Another unhappy person no doubt, because you don't hit somebody just like that, out of the blue. There do exist fairly happy people, though, who are capable of lashing out and striking someone, only to think about it much later, a day later, or two days, maybe a year. They may feel ashamed of their behavior, awkward, possibly monstrously so, but what can you do? They'll remain forever with their thoughts. Yet sometimes they do find a distraction.

Still, they usually think about the incident constantly. As if somebody hit a switch, a grounding switch. Every day this person wakes up in the morning and decides: "Enough is enough! Today is the first day of the rest of my life. I'm going to stop thinking about what drives me up the wall, makes my guts churn, shakes the gray matter out of my ears. These thoughts are making me crazy! Enough is enough! I'm not going to think about it anymore. Why the long face, you dumbass, it happens to everybody. You suffered, now get over it. Today is the first day of the rest of my life, a life where I attain success, where I overcome myself. Brooding over it isn't going to help anybody. It's not going to heal any bruises if I go on beating my breast."

If only everything was as easy at that! Such brave thoughts rarely help anyone. I once heard that pangs of conscience caused a certain fairly decent guy to completely lose it.

I've never felt any sense of security in Ukraine. Even in our Sumy, though it's not as big a city as Kyiv or Kharkiv. It wasn't safe for a girl or woman there, especially if she was walking home in the evening, even if she lived in the city center.

But what can you do? The Sumy Region is in the outer reaches of Ukraine, and the Yampil District, where I come from, is a small district located close to the border, at the edge of the region. Nobody cares about us.

It must have been partisan country out there, way back when. Utter lawlessness, with forests all around, thick forests, impenetrable, enticing. You could do whatever comes to mind, right on the border.

"I feel like weeping," my cousin says, "when I think of the forests." But I, too, can't stay calm when I remember the forests. Our mortal forests are being carted off now, without right or consequence. Trucks and vans usually drive at night, when it's dark, or very early. They're acting illegally, dealing in contraband!

Oh, there used to be such wonderful forests near my home. It was like you could fall into such a forest, fall into it like onto a pillow, so clean the forest was, so peaceful. Sometimes you feel really awful but you go into the forest and you feel better at once.

Sometimes my friends ask who's cutting the forests down. But they're just cutting them down, that's all. How are we to know who's cutting them down? Trucks, cars, carts, all loaded up, driving nights and early in the morning. The more woodchips in the air, the less forest there is to see. Who's behind all of this remains unclear.

One time my aunt was walking by my side, talking about the forest, telling stories, explaining, without saying anything coherent. The main issue that always outrages us is that the forest is going for peanuts. I don't know for how much, but it's definitely not the right price for a forest like that.

How familiar I am with our forests: so boundless they are, dense and dark! But the last time I rode past them, I saw vast clearings, where every tree had been taken out root and branch.

I remember an incident: This guy went off to uproot the forest, a guy I knew from our village, and he really worked hard at the job. He became an affluent man, wouldn't say hello to anybody, walked around with his nose in the air, turned insolent and full of rage. Started raking it in, so he thought he must be some kind of superman. But then he drove into the forest for a walk and he never came back.

You walk and walk and you want to do something so bad when you see all those carts with the tree trunks and the branches sweeping the dust, so thin and helpless. We give everything away in Ukraine. Hey! Has anybody not gotten enough of anything? I used to say, "You didn't make it into the forest yet!" But now they've made it into the forest.

And the villages in the area, the villages! Each house was finer than the next, but now all of them have fallen apart. Once in the middle of the forest there used to be a rich village, huge, wired for electricity, a model for other villages. My grandma and grandpa told me about it. Now there's no trace of it left. Three hovels deep in the woods with an old woman living in each one, picking plants and casting old spells.

Nothing's going to materialize in the village out of thin air. Everybody should understand that. There once were flourishing villages in Ukraine, and some do remain. There are villages in the Kharkiv Region where investments were made, gas put in, electricity, but in our villages they invested nothing. That's how they treated us. And nobody was surprised.

We're almost on the border, basically in the forest, that's why. Nobody really cares about what we do, and on the border you do whatever you want.

And they drive right past us, the trucks—train cars practically. Men from who knows where boom, buzz, uproot, cut, hack, because somebody finds it profitable. But you can hardly get out of the village nowadays. My aunt lives in Shostka and she visits my grandma in the village.

The bus used to stop four times a day at grandma's village; then, when I was in school, it went twice a day, and now, they say, it sometimes won't even come once a day. So how can you leave the village? How can you make it to work?

Another one of our villages, by a last-minute stroke of luck, got connected to a gas line. The village became more respectable right away. Some young people stayed, and others returned.

It's not at all like that in my grandma's old village. She used to tell me about it when I was little: What a village it once was! Flourishing, light-filled, colorful, deep in the forest! But now the people who live there don't know what to do with themselves. Suicide—oh, yes, the only field where youth can show what they're made of, apply themselves, and exercise their imagination. Suicide—the one thing they can make theirs.

There were so many suicides it's tough to remember all of them. When I started studying at the university, one of the students my age hanged himself, another was killed at night, a third drank grain alcohol on a bet and followed the other two. I sometimes ask my aunt what's new in our village. She says in reply, "The neighbor woman on Lenin street passed away, another, even younger, hanged herself, the third went into the forest and never returned." They're all my age or a bit older.

The girl who hanged herself, she was younger than me by about six years. She was really beautiful. Sometimes

I think it was her curse to be so beautiful. There were so many cigarette butts on the ground where she hanged herself, butts strewn all around. I knew her from school. You can always come up with a reason but still, it's a kind of plague we have around here, people killing themselves.

Some come to ruin with drink, of course. Others take poison or do something else. Those are the villages we have. That's the fate they're marked by.

Now the main problem is you can't get out of the area. My brother recently went to visit our grandma; it started to snow heavily, the roads and paths quickly disappeared. He had planned to leave grandma's place at five, but then decided to leave at one p.m.! Why did you spend so little time with grandma, you heartless guy? That's the question. But it was a lucky thing he left so early. The bus came at one, unannounced and unscheduled; the road was already covered with snow; some people were carted out of the village, but others were left behind.

When I was studying at the university, I still lived on occasion with relatives in different villages. Wherever I stayed in the Sumy Region, whether it was in winter or fall, the electricity often went out without warning. Sometimes the lights would go on at night, and people got ready for work. Complete darkness at five p.m., and suddenly the lights come on for a couple of hours. I was a student teacher at a local school. I had to choose: What was I to do that winter evening—make myself something to eat or prepare for classes tomorrow?

Us younger folk suffered with the lights out. Sometimes we'd walk around the streets for hours. You couldn't read, you couldn't do your homework, and there really wasn't anything worth studying, either. We walked around and talked with each other for hours, fantasized, made plans for the future.

Here, where I live now, nobody understands any of it. There's no one I can explain to what it's like for the lights to go out every day in a small village. How we sat around as if inside a bunker, warming ourselves by a bonfire when we managed to light one. How we were next to one another knowing that, in time, all of us would go our separate ways. We huddled against each other by the fire, but later we forgot who we sat next to, what kind of children they were, what kind of people.

It's hard to find your place in life. Some people, though, have a knack for it. Wherever they appear, everybody immediately starts running around them, offering various opportunities. They're settled before they enter a new apartment. They're always the ones picked even out of ten candidates. Sometimes I think it would be good to be this kind of person. You wake up and you have everything under control. You nonchalantly choose what you're going to do; you have breakfast and you go outside to take care of business. But me—I don't even know if I should board this tram or wait for the next one. So I'm sitting at the stop, thinking, "Maybe I should sit here a little longer, spend some time here, give myself a break, take care of myself a bit, after all."

CHRONICLE OF A REVOLT

From a conversation with Katerina N.

In 2015, in the course of judicial proceedings against hairstylists, manicurists, and other workers at the Pyramid Beauty Salon, the examining magistrates, if they may be styled as such, voiced a question that, for the government of the city-state of Anthracite, ought to have cleared up, if only a little, the causes of the revolt.

The examining magistrates inquired after the fashion by which mutinous ideas and thoughts grew and took root in the heads of the beauty salon workers. This question was interestingly answered by Xenia Semyonovna, one of the leaders of the revolt, senior specialist in men's hair arrangement, also known city-wide as master of the Pageboy and the A-line bob styles.

"We recently saw, each of us saw, no one missed any of it, how many townships have been disturbed,

homes turned upside down, women left to litter the road,
frightening passersby with their uncleaned bodies, how
many conquests and reconquests had been carried out
in the name of freedom and independence. We've seen
it all—the Miners' Revolution, the Orange Revolution,
the Revolution of Dignity, and our own Anthracite
Revolution. We've witnessed the making of deeds and
the acquiring of titles: somebody transferred the title of
the stables in the village of Dyakovo; somebody appro-
priated the deed of the municipal market and two gas
stations. But we're broad-minded people—we've never
been petty. They want the gas station? They can have the
gas station. They come to get their hair done but show
us no respect—it's on their own conscience. That was
how our minds took everything in and we, too, learned
to arrange revolutions."

Xenia Semyonovna's address alluded to the political
and military events that deeply disturbed the daytime
and nighttime routines of Anthracite, in consequence of
which the city briefly seceded from the Luhansk Region, as
well from the newly formed state of the Luhansk People's
Republic, to become a state unto itself, ruled by a Cossack
host with atamans at the head.

In all probability, reasoned the examining magistrates,
after a series of events which will probably not be men-
tioned here at all, Xenia Semyonovna herself and her entire
beauty salon fell party to the changes that were taking
place right in front of their eyes. At some point it even
became evident that the Pyramid Beauty Salon was not the
sole organization to grow aware of the necessity of change.
An entire series of other hairdressing establishments, a

fitness center, and two supermarkets in the neighborhood also opted for mutiny! We have yet to investigate all this in the most meticulous fashion, to draw up a court record, and to do everything conceivable, everything that lies within our human reach, to ensure that such events do not repeat. It is not the right time to be lenient with the likes of Xenia Semyonovna.

All the same, it does not seem possible to describe Xenia Semyonova as a mutineer or revolutionary in the classical understanding of these words. After all, ordinary mutineers, viz. the Ukras, the Bandera Bandits, or simply the Dissatisfied, create an environment of their own. They tear themselves away from the rest of city people, turn inward, immerse themselves fully in what they do, take to procuring unauthorized flags from who knows where and addressing each other in prohibited languages. They

often walk out on their families, stop seeing loved ones, rupture relations with their habitual milieu.

Yet Xenia Semyonovna and the workers of her salon never disengaged from their environment. They went about their business, cut hair, manicured nails; they knew many people in town and socialized with anyone fate carried into their salon. Their readiness for mutiny did not contradict their usual way of life; each of them maintained that she wished to make Anthracite *better*. Whose patronage and influence the city found itself under was supposedly a question that lost all meaning for them. They insisted that they had risen *above politics*.

Nonetheless, for all the rebels' shared if rather vaguely defined ideas, they still had not developed a single ideology, whose emergence, as any schoolchild knows, is a requirement for revolutionary organizations. Neither the enhanced interrogations, nor the scrupulous study of the social networks of the detainees, have disproved that hypothesis. The arrested women entertained a rather broad range of opinions. They had received entirely different educations and owned up to an astonishing variety of preferences and perceptions of life and the world. The beauty salon workers included a former student from the department of philosophy of the University of Luhansk, an accountant, an actress, a professional pastry chef, only one professional manicurist but several certified master hairstylists, who, moreover, belonged to different and even mutually hostile schools and traditions of the art. Some of the salon workers composed fluent letters, open or personal, in which they swore never to repeat such a truly fatal mistake, and requested in emotional tones to be let out of the cellar and returned to their families, to their husbands and children. But others—especially the two sisters, Angelica and Albina—wrote with the crudest solecisms, unable to adequately express a single thought. Constantly straying into old, petty squabbles, they argued that they had been systematically underpaid for haircuts for several months already, and that, if it were not for that constant humiliation, they never would have helped Xenia Semyonovna, even though she stood godmother to their children.

It is thereby evident that rebel ranks harbored representatives of well-known and respectable families in Anthracite, as well as entirely unknown women from the provinces, who had moved to Anthracite from adjoining villages in search of a better life.

Nevertheless, they all clearly desired to undertake some activity in the name of either the future of Anthracite, or its present. This readiness of theirs invited suspicion, making them stand out among the other inhabitants of the city.

And yet, in the course of this investigation, the distance that is usually in evidence between apprehended or captured enemies and their examiners did not arise between the rebels and the Cossack specialists from the Anthracite secret services.

There was no class barrier.

For example, a fascinating contradiction was observed in the case of the said Xenia Semyonovna. Her husband, Stoyan Sergeyevich, codename "The Appropriator," was an independent soldier, militia man, amateur martial artist, and activist for the sovereignty of Anthracite and its secession as a city-state.

He conducted agitation among the students of the Professional High School of Automotive Transport, exhorting them to join the Managed Spring Movement and the battles for the city's independence. He furthermore served as the personal consultant of the highly respected ataman Kozitsyn, a man capable of wide-ranging, historically informed ratiocination. Finally, due to his gifts in the field of diplomacy, he often traveled to Donetsk and Luhansk in order to establish intergovernmental-communication relations for Anthracite.

Stoyan Sergeyevich—the very same individual!—abetted the people's cause with all his considerable talents, yet did not notice the alien elements under his own nose, in his own family, a fact he subsequently deeply bemoaned.

Stoyan Sergeyevich's statement of contrition became a key event in the court proceedings against the mutineers. Indeed, for its breadth as well as for the profundity of the issues touched upon, his repentance eclipsed the verdict and sentence, the justice and humanity of which astonished even the issuing magistrates, who did not expect of themselves a corresponding delicacy toward the enemy, manifested moreover at a moment of historical significance for the city-state, as it pursued a war of liberation against two townships, several neighboring city-states, and states properly speaking.

Gravestones used in 1996 to pay back wages to Novovolynsk mine workers. The remains of these wages can still be found on the grounds of one of the mines to this day.

THE POWER OF TIME

Native Americans have long black hair that looks like wings and hangs down straight in an indissoluble stream. Xenia also has long black hair. Native Americans, as everyone knows, were once not afraid of anything—they were masters of secret knowledge. Xenia also is fearless and a master of certain knowledge.

Native Americans recognized kindness for many miles around. They knew very well if there might be some nice person someplace in the badlands, even if they were very far away. Even if they wouldn't meet up with them, still they knew! Xenia often thought about Native Americans.

She spent the great part of each day in the metro, inside the Leo Tolstoy, Independence Square, and Contract Square stations. She walked up and down the platform, sometimes going into the train cars, offering various minor goods to the passengers. She liked to sell markers most. To make her business more successful she made up several brief and convincing speeches. I cite one of them in full:

"Excellent two-sided markers!

"They highlight the main idea! They highlight a word or a letter! They will help focus your attention on what really matters.

"Universal markers! You can sign your name with them. They draw on metal or glass.

"Astonishing, amazing colorful markers for writing or drawing! Pick them up once and you'll never put them down. They cost almost nothing, mere kopeks. Just try one and you'll lose your mind! You'll want to buy every color!"

Xenia was convinced this was the job that suited her best. Three or four times a week she met with her wholesaler, who gave her markers, pens, scotch tape, and notepads to sell on consignment. They met at a small market near Sevastopol Square and, because the wholesaler was a man of few words, their meetings usually transpired in total silence.

He received a few hundred hryvni from Xenia and, in return, passed her multicolored shafts wrapped in paper or transparent tape. The sober and tight-lipped air of their transaction must have made it look illegal. Their chance witness, the man behind the book table, regarded them with reproach and suspicion. His mistrustful and astonished stare excited Xenia.

She would walk off, her shoulder pleasantly pulled down by the strap of her bag filled with markers and notepads, which didn't feel heavy at all. Xenia liked to leave the market and walk over to the informal street market nearby, where eggs and chicken carcasses lay on open newspapers, one-liter glass jars held fresh milk, and fruit was sold either by piece or by weight, but always at affordable prices. Two rows of unregulated traders exchanged shouts across the aisle. Envoys constantly embarked to their neighbors or to the other row in search of change. An echoing hum rose above the street market. Negotiations carried on everywhere at once.

Xenia would stroll back and forth along the rows, buy some trifle, and then head for the metro. Lately, she often thought about how she might sneak into the metro by some different, nonstandard entrance. She didn't like to pay the fare, as she didn't go anywhere anyway—so she reasoned to herself—didn't travel to other places, and usually left the metro by the same station she had entered.

If she wasn't in the metro, wasn't seeing train cars depart into the blackness of the tunnel, nor the thinning crowds hurrying to the exit or the connecting train, she would be seized with anxiety.

Only the noise of the metro had the power to soothe this restless soul.

Only the metro gave her a feeling of comfort, warmth, protection, and, yes, love. Nothing in her life was better or worse than the metro.

She was especially enraptured with stations that lay two escalators below street level. Riding on escalators gave Xenia great pleasure. She liked to raise up two fingers, a gesture that signified: "It's a tailwinds kind of day today!" She liked to remember the descents down the steep slopes of ski resorts, which she often saw advertised on the digital screens inside train cars.

One day a woman in a train car gave her a stern look, and Xenia ran to a mirror at the station, so that the reflection might take the force of that look away. She felt that a curse had been placed on her. She was probably right because she barely made it to the mirror. Her heart had begun beating more slowly, and there was a huge wave of sadness about to swallow her.

With feigned indifference the mirror reflected the rails at a slant, as if inviting her to look into the tunnel. Xenia stood as close as possible to the yellow line, which may not be crossed when the train is arriving, and looked into the mirror. She saw her face slightly curved by the crooked glass. A far-off rumbling signaled the approach of a train. A gust of air hit her back, like at the onset of a big storm. Flattened colorful shadows poured into the train-car doors. Then the doors closed with a ringing sound, and car after car rushed past Xenia, carrying away not only the curse, but all the other sorrows that had vexed her over the last two years.

ELENA

On April 4, 2017, Elena realized that she couldn't talk with her mother any longer. It was a decision she made while riding the bus from Manganese to Dnipropetrovsk. She took this complicated and onerous trip twice a week because she lived in Manganese, where her job hardly paid anything. In Dnipropetrovsk she worked in what she figured was an upscale restaurant—as an assistant chef—and they paid her so generously that it covered the trip and afforded her a few pleasant trifles. She started rereading magazines that insistently recommended "making time to pamper yourself." Exactly how she was going to pamper herself is what she contemplated on the bus. Maybe she would go to a beauty salon near her work. Maybe she would buy herself the red and orange coat that she hadn't yet dared try on; or she could start saving money and one day carry out those home repairs, or perhaps move to Dnipropetrovsk. But what sort of move could she be thinking of if her mother lived in Manganese and had no desire to leave?

Elena again started thinking about her mother. The thought frightened her right away. Frightened her first and foremost because she didn't resemble her mother enough. Her mother once worked in a narrow-fabric weaving factory, the biggest in Europe, a legend in their town. "There is no kind of ribbon that our factory didn't make," she would say. Mama was a great expert in ribbons; she knew the difference between binding and moire ribbons. She could tell color nuances apart and understood perfectly well which ribbon was specifically used for what. Ever since she was a child Elena had wanted to have the same occupation as her mother, or possibly surpass her—to become a weaver, a seamstress, or a ribbon designer. What can be better than a ribbon? A ribbon so long you could tie it around the Earth, that's how long it is. Then the Earth would resemble one great, big gift set you could offer somebody—somebody more attentive and caring.

Usually when Elena boarded the bus, she took out a small black cellphone and dialed a familiar number.

"Yes, Mama, I'm on the bus. I got on safely, the bus wasn't late. The driver is pleasant, not drunk, the other passengers are polite, too. I'm on my way. It's fine."

When Elena arrived in Dnipropetrovsk she would call her mother again.

"Mama, I'm already in Dnipropetrovsk. We arrived safely. I'm on my way to work now. I'm going to be held up tonight, we need to bake a few cakes for some fancy party. A man came to see us, he was witty, well-dressed, and he ordered cakes. Can you imagine, they're supposed to say 'Our Magical Summer,' 'Dreams Come True,' and 'You Are My Girl Queen.' That's how openhanded these Dnipropetrovsk people are. When they give presents, they give presents. We don't have people like that."

When Elena walked into the restaurant, she would have to call her mother again, or her mother called her.

"Hi, Mama! It's very hot at work. Lots of noise—I'm not alone here. It smells sweet, you would like it. Yes, that man took the cakes, I even brought them out to him myself. He said I was like a tender flower or something like that, but it was beautiful how he said it. No, I'm not thinking about him. Of course I didn't give him my number, just like you taught me. I'm thinking only about work, but it was nice that he said it. It's because you're my mama and you're so beautiful that he was nice to me. I take after you, of course. Bye, Mama. I am leaving for home soon, in five hours."

In short, Elena frequently called her mother and tried to be as similar to her in life as possible. She always had her mother on her mind and she thought there could be no better woman in the world. But at some point, namely on April 4, 2017, Elena suddenly felt that she couldn't call Manganese, that she simply couldn't hear her mother's voice. She felt she loved her so much that she couldn't endure talking to her anymore. She thought that even the briefest conversation would be unbearable.

The narrow-fabric weaving factory had turned into gorgeous ruins, where she and her mother loved to go for a stroll together.

The townspeople no longer knew how to produce ribbons. People quickly unlearned what they once knew, and only Elena's mother held on to the memory of her art, sometimes looking over her old workbooks and production plans.

Elena would never be able to continue her mother's work. People have changed very rapidly around them. Her mother's close friends, women who used to be employed at the factory, now don't want to hear of it. They have all found other jobs, or have moved from Manganese to Dnipropetrovsk, or to Zaporizhia.

Elena felt the ground slowly giving way beneath her feet. She wasn't even able to preserve the manner of speaking that she had received from her mother. Each new person in Elena's life forced her to speak otherwise, to pronounce her *g* the hard way, although her mother preferred the soft Ukrainian *g*, almost a *kh*.

How long can you take it?! Life keeps flying by, every new person we meet consumes our thoughts and displaces those we love from our minds. Each new day rides roughshod over the one before it. Fine, so be it!

Perhaps Elena was so devoted to her mother, loved her city so much, that she could no longer endure that simple and nonetheless unbearable fact that her mother's voice gradually sank into oblivion as soon as she left Manganese for a day. And as for Manganese itself, nobody there wanted to remember anything either.

Her name, which Elena thought far more beautiful than herself, also belonged to her mother. It was what Mama and her girlfriends privately called the dark blue ribbon that they began to produce in the beginning of the eighties.

As Elena kept thinking, her capacity to continue on as before vanished; her patience popped like a balloon.

On April 4, 2017, she threw her phone into a fountain, spent the night in the store room of the restaurant, and the following day requested a seven-day workweek. She asked them for whatever terms but they immediately offered her a higher salary. She was prepared to sleep in the train station but they suggested she live the first month for free in the unoccupied apartment owned by the bookkeeper.

This is how Elena started living and working in Dnipro.

THE CRASH

Time flows imperceptibly in our café, in the rhythm of music. I wish I could learn to be totally unaware of the passing of life. To take no notice of time, however absurd that might sound. After all, I just said that it passes imperceptibly, like the first nocturnal snowfall of the year. Time steals by.

I can't feel it, and it knows nothing about me. We dwell in separate spaces. It perches on clock dials, but I'm set at liberty, completely free of any obligations toward it.

There's not a single thing I would do on time.

There's not a single completed task that I could full-heartedly consider over and done with, not a single memory to arise before me with clarity and precision.

I've learned to rid myself of worries. After certain carefully selected exercises, I've also rid myself of memory.

I think that the clocks on the walls don't remember anything, and that time is an empty fiction made up by the windbags who aspire to organize their lives and those of others.

I don't know how old I am.

I have no idea how to describe the reality around me.

But I want to talk—not sure how yet or what about, just to talk. To pronounce words, as if each word, taken separately, could be a substantial thing, a significant thing. They are my loyal knights—words in emptiness, words unsupported by any event that has ever happened, words stripped of history.

I like the form of a word—rounded as an empty glass, a vessel bereft of meaning.

I like the sound of a word—a corridor echoing with other words, whose origins drown in the dark depths of the sea.

At that very moment, right in front of me, there suddenly rises a circular face with protruding ears. My new acquaintance. He demands a small glass of vodka and a lemon. He smacks his creased lips, licks them quickly, in haste, leaving a thin strip of moisture on his pale, furrowed upper lip, and fixes his gaze at the shining bar.

The day will come when sorrow will send a smile my way.

That's what an acquaintance used to tell me, and why shouldn't he come to mind now. Now that the day passes without having started; now that it is ending without having so much as considered giving birth to an event.

My acquaintance was sort of even my friend. We saw each other often; I went over to his house after school, his parents usually wouldn't be home, and I would lie down on the couch, raise my legs against the rug that decorated, or rather protected, the wall. There, I would learn to circumscribe with my eyes the gyres of the arbori-form design. The geometric pattern of opening petals and black-cored circumferences distracted me from the feeling of sadness, from my not wanting to stay at my friend's for the night but also from my fierce hatred of my family and my home, which I did not want to go back to.

Now the visitor focuses more deeply on the partition, the glistening surface of the bar counter, where he's prob-ably looking for his reflection. But I search for myself and my future among shadows cast by tables and displaced wooden chairs.

A strong, forceful arm flashes before my eyes and then settles in the rectangle of my vision. The owner of our café counts the earnings, fills his pockets with crumpled banknotes, roughly half the contents of the cash register, mutters something unintelligible, and vanishes.

A wave of air—compressed, completely alien, numb, sodden with booze—crashes over me. For a moment I can't breathe, my head is spinning, but I come to my senses.

Today, like many other people, I am where I am and I see before me several uncomplicated tasks for the day and I am ready for them. Yet idleness, along with my more sophisticated and consistent inertia, may at some point kill me, deprive me of even that trifle that I managed to conquer from life.

The visitor doesn't move. He is sad; his inviolability appears to recall some past personal misfortune. But it may possibly be that he doesn't feel anything and has turned into a cliff, into the doorman guarding my evening. In that case I allow him to attack with fierce shouts another casual visitor driven into our establishment by the wind and rain. He doesn't touch the vodka that I amiably set next to the crook of his elbow. I thought I had successfully calculated the energy he would require to reach the glass as well as to empty it.

Wild roses, red roses, might have bloomed in this café! Then each alcoholic, wishing to come to for a moment, would have been able to scratch his palm with their thorns to contemplate the droplets of blood numbly gliding along the lifeline.

But all we have are a few barely living ficus stretching their emaciated branches toward the tin shades of dull lamps in a farewell gesture before they die.

The real purpose behind our café was to open a strip club in its place. It would be one of the cheapest in town. It would have a private entrance, so that only certain nouveau-riche taxi drivers, long-distance truckers, journalists, and office workers might earn the honor of being called our regular, beloved, and deeply esteemed visitors.

But the era of strip clubs in our neighborhood ended almost as soon as it began. A certain Guardian of Public Order, a never sober yet highly influential servant of the law, came to see us last week. He instructed the owner to throw his dreams and ambitions as far away as they would fly, since our street is inhabited by reputable people, whose family members are entirely ignorant of the fact that, in our town, striptease offers the only opportunity for an evening establishment to make rather than eke out a living.

Will we never amount to anything? Will we always remain what we have already turned into, after numerous renovations and remodelings: a barely heated kiosk trading in moonshine?

THE SHILLYSHALLIER

Prorizna—the slit—is a street in Kyiv I've been afraid of my whole life. There was a school here a good friend of mine used to go to when she was very little. A bony, round-faced boy punched her in the stomach in the school yard many years ago. Nobody noticed anything. They were alone, just the two of them: he and she. He looked her in the eye, wanting to say something, then changed his mind. She was in pain but not so much pain, actually. Average pain. She decided immediately that she wouldn't think about the incident, wouldn't hit him back, wouldn't remember his name. And that's almost how it happened. She never managed to push the episode itself out of her head. She still thinks about it, recalls the pleasant sensation of time slowing down to let the mind follow the diminishing pain at leisure. As for the street, she still prefers to steer clear of it, though not because of the incident but for no apparent reason at all, she says. Plus there are many other ways to walk up from the Khreshchatyk to Volodymyrska Street and the Golden Gate.

I, too, am sure of it: The Slit is an entirely unreliable street. Anyone may easily experience any sort of trouble here. It slices through the hill, stitching down from the Golden Gate to the Khreshchatyk, where nobody ever gets any rest, day or night, evening or morning.

Yet chance brought me to the Slit again, for all my resistance.

I again was looking for something to do, again because I had no idea what to do with my life. There are all sorts of things you can do: You can help people eat more, or you can help them become more beautiful, or happier. You also can live more modestly, without ideals, by taking care of yourself and your loved ones, first and foremost. At present I am trying to hold down an occupation that combines these possibilities. Who am I? After all of my worries and searches, I am now an unassuming but very diligent custodian and saleswoman who works in a stone shop. Or rather it's not so much that I work here but that I want to work here. They hired me on a trial basis. We sell semiprecious stones. We take product selection seriously. Malachite alone we sell in thirty varieties. We have many kinds of amber, even a dried-blood-brown type that recalls a withered rose.

True, barely anyone buys our stones. The store is there; customers do come in. But they visit mainly to share their troubles, to talk about what keeps them up at night, rather than to buy stones.

Our boss is a genius! He knows how to make money even under these conditions. He never so much as hints at being upset. For days the shop stays empty of customers, but he still rubs his hands contentedly. He is a man with the mind of a chess master. I try to learn from him every day, every minute. Believe me, he dwells on a far higher plane than a regular salesman. He has reached an uncommon state—that of total indifference to everything. The world, ruled as it is by special essences, energy balancers guzzling down the energy of fools, cannot subdue such a man. The world retreats every time it nears him, as if it were crashing on a rock.

Today a fair-haired woman walked into the store—to admire the opals we set out in a glass case. I know her very well! She is a member of our city intelligentsia. There was a time when she worked in the accounts department of the opera house. Then she made her name and capital for decades by cleaning the apartments of French embassy staff. She had connections in Europe. She spent years building herself a private home with two fireplaces just outside Kyiv, and only now is it nearly finished. In the meantime, this woman came to hone her taste and sense of form by contemplating our stones.

Or maybe not. She was worried about something, oppressed by something that gave her no rest. She asked for our owner several times, whether he'd come in today to check the books. The owner sometimes sees customers in a separate director's office, but today he wasn't in Kyiv, I couldn't promise her anything. Her face abruptly pulled very close to mine and she covered her wrinkled lips with her hand, whispering: "Trypillia stone. He promised to give me the Trypillia stone. Maybe he hid it somewhere around here, do you know?"

I couldn't do anything for her. She heaved a sigh and shared her affliction with me. Her only son, she said, is a man of extraordinary beauty. He is almost forty but doesn't look older than twenty-five. Not a spot of gray. From afar, his posture resembles that of a politician. From up close, he may be mistaken for a hero of ancient legends and tales. Even in our difficult times he has managed to retain the innocence of an infant. But the world can be merciless toward people like that. The son fell into the wrong hands, and my interlocutor, after trying all possible remedies, resolved to act on her last option. She would try to do away with her daughter-in-law.

It was a difficult decision for her, a believer. But a son is a son. You would clench your teeth for his sake, and *commit an act*, no matter how unsightly. How is it possible to go on tolerating such things? How to tolerate rudeness, vulgarity, incompetence in housekeeping, the gluttony of the daughter-in-law, and especially the fact that she always was and will now remain an entirely ailing individual? She has no health. Wherever she goes, a giant bag full of medicines goes with her, and she insolently gulps down pills by the handful. She pours a tablespoon of pills down her maw right in front of everyone. She doesn't even drink them down with water.

To die, the daughter-in-law must listen to the fully charged Trypillia stone only a few times. It's also important that she be in a special state of mind: the state of mind that could be called "traditional." The owner of our shop took pity on this refined, educated woman who suffered so, and he saved a stone for her. The Trypillia must be carried home on your bosom with care, under your dress, so as not to damage it, so that the stone doesn't recalibrate its vector of influence.

Unfortunately the owner wasn't in today. He didn't leave any stone for anyone, and we didn't dare call him.

I didn't know how to help this woman, who thrashed about in front of the counter like a wounded dove. In the end I manufactured a few warm reassuring words for her, and she started to smile. It's surprising but I often manage to reassure people and make them happy. A good psychologist—one customer said that about me, and it's true.

I know how to choose the right words at the right time, to utter them unobtrusively and softly, and then the person is already happy, smiling, ready to venture forth and joyfully fulfill her cherished desires and dreams. It is important in life to discover your innate abilities at the right time and start developing them. But I still can't make up my mind what I'm going to be in the future. You can do different things in life, you can reach the summit by constantly moving forward, or you can stay a shillyshallier like me for years. This particular, lamentable fate awaits me, I fear. What matters is not to be afraid, but to act. But how to act if you don't know which way to go and where to start?

THE STARS

The days drag on with no meaning. It's really quiet in A, where we live. Nobody shoots at anybody; nobody asks for explanations for no reason; roadblocks don't work the way they do at B. Here, you can drive through a roadblock unmolested, especially if you are taking a jitney bus or taxi.

I don't orient myself well in the city where I've spent my whole life.

I don't understand who these people are: the ones I consider my friends, the ones I get together with every Thursday to play cards for small change while consuming a mountain of cookies and candy. What scares me most is stability. There's a quiet, but an unsteady kind of quiet, giving way, like a bog or a swamp. That's it, a swamp. Not a soul around. I am searching for my husband in the forest, in the middle of water, knee-deep. Did this happen to me? Or did none of it happen? You're going to laugh. It happened not to me but to my neighbor. For some reason

I always find myself in her place when I tell her story. Don't chalk me up for crazy. I often have dreams that I'm by a line of trees, gallons of blood running everywhere, a cart completely covered with bodies, they're shooting us down, a firing squad. It must have come from a history textbook. I have nothing left to do but to climb into the cart, hide under the bodies, and smear blood over my face so that they count me as one of the dead.

Whereas in real life, rather than in a dream, here's what happened. Last year, my neighbor went searching for her husband—they had taken him prisoner, but then they said they had let him go. She searched for him day after day for many days, and in the end found him in the forest! It took a while. She started in the nearby villages, then she searched in town, and then at his relatives' places. Finally, she took to wandering around the forest, calling him by name until he answered. The forest is a good place to shout out somebody's name. You can even howl.

They held hands and walked through our vast forest. Whenever I remember my neighbor's story the forest strikes me as impenetrable, gigantic. The trees of the forest rose high above them like ship masts. Sergey, her husband, walked beside her; they moved very lightly, with cushioned tread, as if they had feathers on their soles, or a layer of moss. She said that the moss in the forest began to understand them. The moss spread out before them and became their compliant ground, carpet, and pillow for their every step, each step so soft no one heard them. They found a path that, in three hours, brought them to a roadway, and from there the town was close at hand. Night had fallen but they nonetheless learned very quickly how to see really well in the dark. And despite the cold they learned not to feel cold.

I learned that, too: how hot my hand has become. A guy I know was riding his bike and saw them, the way they were walking on the road, but he didn't stop. Many people say that the most important thing for us is to have peace. But I'm going to say to you that peace doesn't matter. Something else matters. But I don't know what. I just know peace isn't it.

While the war was going on I felt calm, because I was living from one shelling to another. I wasn't living day by day, but minute by minute and hour by hour. My friends were with me. No matter what they talked about, their words lacked any kind of importance. In those troubled hours and days their words were inaudible. Once uttered, they became objects, things—something solid and possessing form rather than meaning.

Right on through the gluey green wall of rain, a neighbor in a blue dress ran to the entryway: ran to save a hen. They called the hen Vika. She survived the war, she became a victor, and so they named her Victoria. The neighbor survived, too. The hen sometimes hid in the basement of our building. She would approach many of us and she lost her fear of human beings. On one of those days the neighbor announced that she couldn't bear it any longer, sitting below ground and guessing about what was going on above—with their house, with that birdbrain Vika. We laughed at our neighbor, at her inability to sit still. Then the neighbor showed us a page from the paper, *The Town News*, and there was a horoscope printed there for each day. Some signs were given hour by hour.

It turned out that Pisces could be sure of their well-being and safety from three to five p.m. that day. And so my neighbor, a pure Pisces without any additions, could easily leave the basement. There might be rumbling somewhere up above but nothing would touch her, almost for certain.

Pisces kept Victoria company, and they had a good time together. Everything felt surprising to me that day and I even believed the rumors it was Canada that was waging war against us—over the discovery of new deposits of valuable coal. Some of us were already deeply convinced of the fact. We sat in the basement thinking about Canadian aggression, about how greedy, vindictive, and heartless other countries could be. "Those bombs are made in Canada," the whisper swirled around the cellar, and for some reason we found it comforting.

We all started to study the horoscope. Scorpio was safe tomorrow from noon until almost evening. That was how I went out for my first stroll. I walked around a city where that was both smoky and bright. The streets were empty, the windows had no glass, the ground seemed to tremble a little, while the thin trees curled down under the weight of their leaves. We've never had such quiet before.

By the dumpster I met an alcoholic I knew. He was totally sober. Like me, he stood there, looking around in surprise. It turned out he was a Scorpio. Naturally his instinct for self-preservation brought him up to the surface. I didn't encounter problems returning to the cellar. We started making calculations so that we may go into town during safe hours. Nothing happened to us—nothing special, nothing terrible—because we always went and came back in the breaks between shooting.

These days I, too, am reading the horoscope. Today, after six and until nine, I'm advised to "seek seclusion and privacy at a time appropriate for reflection and best spent at home." This can be interpreted as saying the time would be unsafe above. Believe it or not, with such veiled recommendations, the horoscope informed our whole building when there would be immediate danger to life during a shelling.

The shelling has been over for a long while now. Still, the horoscope keeps giving the same recommendations, the wording unchanged, but we no longer understand it.

The stars used to be on our side: you might say they worked for us. Now it's as if everything has broken down, the sky does whatever the sky wants. Time has turned its back on our city. There's nothing happening.

TRANSFORMATIONS

We met up in Sloviansk, where she stopped by for several days. She wanted to, as she put it, "get a breath of fresh air" so sorely lacking for her in Kyiv during the May holidays.

Kyiv empties out on those days. A completely empty city: some late mornings you go out into the street and find no one there. The sun bleaches the trees so that only their contours are visible. One building can barely be told apart from another. "I don't see so well in the bright sun anymore. Sunrise frightens me. My innards clench up at dawn and I wake up."

Her name was Olga, friends called her Olga Petrovna because that's what she preferred. "There's a measure of respect you feel in the patronymic," she explained. "The first name, if unaccompanied, exists somehow off on its own and doesn't aspire to much. Ever since I was a child I didn't want to be called by my first name alone. I felt being called by your given name was literally being called out by your name: 'Hey, Nastya, c'mere!,' or 'Lyuda, tell the class what the answer is.' Slowly, inevitably, the resentment builds up.

"But with a patronymic it's like you're not alone, there are people behind you, rooting for you, and you're the foremost among them.

"I don't like first names to be solitary, without a patronymic and family name, and I can't stand the city when it's empty. An empty city violates the order of things. It's an infringement on who you're, a mockery that might possibly suggest a natural disaster though it's never an appropriate suggestion.

"The emptiness feels as if some dismal, implausible creature might break the surface at any moment. Something rational but inhuman, covered in fur, with nails sharp as knives, armed with barbaric laughter. The creature would open its maw and burst into laughter—not the laughter of an individual but of a huge, drunken crowd, angry and frenzied, a serpentine multitude of feminine cackles and masculine titters.

"Kyiv empties out without warning. On Cossack Street, where I rent my apartment, life became extinct. I went out to get milk in the early morning of the first of May and there wasn't a soul on the street, the stores closed, although the windows weren't nailed shut nor the glass shielded with plywood."

Olga Petrovna didn't live alone in Kyiv. She rented a corner in a three-room, owner-occupied apartment. Her former neighbors from the unassuming township of Happy Mountain lived with her in the same room.

"I don't live alone, I rent a corner, as they say. Three of us together in one room but the two others, the married couple Oleg Nikolayevich and Anna Sergeyevna, went away the day before yesterday and left me on my own.

"Probably not the best idea to leave me alone. When I'm by myself I start to see what nobody sees and hear what nobody hears. I perform impossible, magical deeds. For example, believe it or not, the day before yesterday I transformed a pot of kasha into a flower. It happened in broad daylight, completely by accident. Transformed into a hydrangea.

"The pot of kasha was on the stove. Oleg Nikolayevich and particularly Anna Sergeyevna didn't think of putting it away, although it was their kasha and they were leaving for a week. There it was on the stove, not bothering anyone, looking pretty in tinsel from New Year's. I got up in the morning, drank a small cup of coffee as I always do in the morning, prepared to go to work, went to the neighbors in our building, cleaned their apartments, cleaned two offices in the building across the street, came home, but it was only three in the afternoon. There was still no end of time before evening, and so I felt the yearning to transform things. I indulged in that pastime before, but just recently I received a refresher course from a new acquaintance, the battalion medicine man, who was stationed near our Happy Mountain.

"The things I did in our room! First I transformed a tablespoon into a wooden Easter egg. Then I picked up another spoon, a tiny one that the whole room of us loved, and I changed it into a blue silk ribbon. But even that felt like it wasn't enough. I transformed this one postcard that we received from the borough congratulating us on International Women's Day—I transformed it into three matches! *That* made my eyes hurt.

"Sometimes you're looking at a thing prior to its transformation: there it is, standing on its own right before you, clean and pure. Then you project the charms at the thing, and you don't even have time to tell what happened but right there's a totally different object before your eyes. The recoil hits your vision, first and foremost. Your heart might start to palpitate. Something in your chest falls silent, you stop breathing, you're looking in front of you, watching how the world alters, holding your breath.

"We had a teapot. A regular teapot, the kind found in many households—white with orange circles. We got ahold of one somehow, by hook or by crook. Anna Sergeyevna, for reasons unknown, felt fear before the teapot, almost a religious terror. For me it was just an everyday object, whereas Oleg Nikolayevich loved the teapot and wouldn't on any account agree to exchange it for a new one. The teapot came with a history, it arrived here from Happy Mountain together with us. And everything would be fine except that every time we fill the teapot with boiling water and offer tea to a guest or to each other, water pours out from the spout and onto the tablecloth, the floor, or the table. Puddles are always forming around the teapot. You have to tilt the pot in a particular way, supporting its side, pouring slowly and with respect, lifting it high, and then less water will spill—you know what I mean. And this was the teapot that—on the ill-fated evening before last—I transformed into a woman's fan. It was by accident. I was coming out of the bathroom, upset because of the spoons, and the teapot appeared right in front of my eyes. At first it just stood there, but then it seemed to advance at me, as if challenging me, like, 'You're not going to do anything to me, you don't have the backbone, you don't have what it takes.'

"But I don't like being insulted for no reason. And who in the whole wide world would endure unjustified humiliation, no matter how insignificant? I became incensed, and at one fell swoop zonked it into a fan. Only the handle from the teapot remained. The fan turned out to have a teapot's handle."

Olga Petrovna cast a bitter glance at the coffee cup she held in her hand just then. She explained to me that she came to Sloviansk in order to rest her soul from her Kyivan misadventures and to prepare herself for a return to an altogether different city than the one she had left two days ago. When she left, Kyiv was utterly empty. She will return in the last days of the May holiday week to an overflowing city, one so filled with various people, smells, and events, that she fears—this she admitted with sadness—there might no longer be found any place for her among those people and events.

From Happy Mountain, where she lived her whole life, she moved in 2014 first to Artemivsk, then to Kharkiv, and from there, very recently, to Kyiv. After the numerous moves she decided to ascertain at least once a week whether she should remain in Kyiv or not. She goes out to her street, strolls to the intersection of Cornflower Street, then strolls back. If she doesn't happen upon certain signs that she must abandon Kyiv, she stays for another week.

Olga Petrovna is a very respectable person. I beg you not to mistake her for the neighborhood madwoman. I don't rule out the possibility that she does possess the uncommon talent of transforming one thing into another and of changing the forms of objects. She wanted to transform a napkin into a tiny homunculus for my sake but, since the waiter wouldn't take his eyes off us, she decided against it.

LILACS

Thunder suddenly rumbled above me and the woman I was talking to. But not a single drop fell from the sky. The thunder turned out to be the first chords of a song I didn't know before. After the thunder the song poured out from the loudspeakers placed in the street. Two rectangular black boxes encased in moss-like cloth transmitted the voices of alien civilizations from their radio-mouths: Soviet, Russian, and American songs.

We were standing on the former Karl Marx Avenue in Dnipro. We met one another not so long ago, though long enough to understand that it would be difficult for us to be around each other. I came here to see Andrea, whom I hadn't heard from for some time, and she was ready to talk about anything except the very reason we were meeting up. Last week Andrea claimed to know a certain secret about the war, its original cause no less, but when we met she behaved as if she had forgotten about her phone call.

A broad and unfamiliar avenue stretched before us. To the right a couple of carousels with bright plastic seats went round and round to the sound of a drumroll. The rotating mechanisms carried soft, yielding children's bodies forward and in a circle; the children laughed and laughed.

Maybe the whole trip was pointless. Standing next to Andrea I often tried to imagine what would have happened if I had been someone else. If, instead of going from town to town with a list of questions, I myself were the paragon, the example, the processed voice illustrating a specific story. But my imagination brought me back to a vacuum where there was nothing, not one point of reference. More and more often I would ask myself during interviews: Where is my listener? Who is he? His hearing fails; he alternates between feelings of horror, hope, and emptiness; he is smothered by the fear that—as he now realizes—it's not possible to say anything about anything.

I wasn't able to focus, but Andrea kept talking, having decided that the time had come for flashy editorializing about Ukraine. At first she sprinkled declarations of love, assuring me that she was in love with the Ukrainian character, but also said, at the same time, that Ukraine is, as she put it, "the land of residual phenomena." Everything noteworthy, significant, and living escapes from Ukraine, so she said, and only the residue remains: restless substances full of longing that by chance found themselves in demand nowhere else, abandoned by the rest of the world. She kept pointing to herself and saying: *I am a microsubstance.*

"Only the smallest particles can survive in Ukraine, a country that leaves its inhabitants very little room for any maneuvering in its practice of humongous fakery and high-stakes play. The drive for freedom is a collective imitation. Maidan, the Revolution of Dignity, the Orange Revolution—each a skillfully staged spectacle. These events weren't real protests, never mind revolutions. They were illusions, the dreams of exhausted people. Exhausted by Europe, by Ukraine, by the memory of the Soviet Union, by the very thought of having to lead an inconspicuous meager life among worlds gaping to swallow them.

"Our real flag," she explained, "is the spot left on the wall by the hammer and sickle. Not the yellow-blue flag, but a white, empty flag showing only the shadows of the hammer and sickle, and of the wheat stalks tied with a red bandage, or else just the line dividing the yellow and the blue—a thin, barely discernible straight line.

"Factories and industrialization cost my parents' parents their lives. But there's no trace left of that industrialization today. We don't have anywhere to work, but it's silly to sigh about it—there's no way we can work the way they used to work, anyway."

It's impossible to follow Andrea: she makes continuous assertions, anxiously swerving from one idea to the next, demanding that everything be recorded and documented exactly, but a minute later she looks over her shoulder and asks me to cross out this or that thought.

"Everything I say—somebody will take note of it. They kept an eye on my parents, although it was more like a half an eye, because my parents were considered the right sort of people, worker class. Both of them were very naive, listened to forbidden radio stations for hours, and thought they knew the world inside and out. I'm completely defenseless next to you. You might be at the employ of Western secret services; you might be an agent, and anyway they could be tailing us and my words could recoil and hurt me badly."

She was glancing around with a histrionic fear while I stupidly desired to justify myself, to explain to Andrea *whose side I am on.*

It's true, Andrea did ask me several times, as if playing a children's game, "Whose side are you on?" There are lots of sides—pick any one. Russia is waging war against Ukraine. Ukraine is waging war against an internal enemy. We are waging war against those who don't understand us. People say that Europe is also waging some kind of war here.

If the story of this meeting does wind up in my book, it will be its most convoluted story—perhaps the one that will be described as the "worst" story. Every dust particle, thingamajig, object, rainwater pipe, children's amusement ride on the avenue must have had a clearer idea of what was going on than I did. What a pointless day.

Andrea asked me to refrain at all costs from describing her appearance, to do everything I could to make her unrecognizable from my description—it would help her to tell me things she wouldn't entrust to anyone else. She wasn't the first person to come to me with this request. But that day, at that moment, I thought that Andrea hid herself from the eyes of others because of excessive modesty. Gradually she adopted the habit of repeating: "How can I possibly matter? Because I don't matter at all. People like me live an inconspicuous life and wilt after a short blooming period, like lilacs." She said that she compared herself to lilac flowers because she used to be so gorgeous that she would avoid looking at herself in the mirror.

"At least this is why it's better for you and me if no one knows about me. I could be called to account, couldn't I? But is there anything I can change? Not only can I not change anything, I don't dare to. You're taking my words down, you must be counting on something. Maybe a tearjerker about how we're all full of hope for a new future, or how the country that we loved became our prison. We're left to eke out a life in small towns, to die in plundered hospitals, in dirty public wards, or in empty little apartments where there's no hot water for months and the lights go out at night. Someone will want to hear about us, and then *you* will be the one invited to a grand festive table, *you* will be the one they'll raise a toast to.

"That's when you'll remember me, how I summoned you to Dnipro to entrust you with a secret, but then I didn't dare tell you anything. Believe me, not out of duplicity or malice, but out of good old fear. An instinctive, animal fear having to do with being recognized, having my features identified, that they will laugh at me, at best, and then they will mock me. Tell me, is that naive? Is that funny or unsophisticated?

"I'm nobody, and I understand that perfectly well. But if you're going to write about me anyway, change everything: name, hair color, or better yet don't mention my appearance at all. Friends and acquaintances could easily recognize me by certain signs, or by things you omit.

"When the soldiers arrived, we didn't know what army they were from, we didn't even know from what direction and why they had come. We lived on the outskirts of the village. I stepped out of the house to help my neighbor. A soldier was standing in front of me. He asked me for water, I led him to the well. I was afraid to look him in the eye. I was walking with my head down, but he still touched my shoulder with his hand several times. Our neighbor's daughter had come to see her parents during her vacation: She was screaming, I heard her calling for me, but for some reason I couldn't run to her rescue. With my hands trembling I turned the wheel of the well, gave him some water to drink. He asked if I knew where they were from, what army, whose side they were fighting on. I didn't know or understand anything. I'm over thirty, but I couldn't understand."

Suddenly she was interrupted by the announcer's voice. The city radio station reported through the loudspeakers: "Today the church of the Renaissance in the city of Dnipro offers a day of prayer for the cure of chronic diseases. And featured later tonight—the long-awaited prayer for the breaking of personal curses! All in the run-up to tomorrow's holiday ministry talk: 'You're Destined for Happiness, Girl!'"

Andrea immediately began persuading me to go to church with her. For a long time, she said, she hadn't been able to find peace, so she had asked me to come meet her. But now that she was talking to a complete stranger who has not lived through anything, she said, she feels better and is finally ready to take care of her soul. Especially since she personally knows a priest without a family. "He is handsome," said Andrea, "and he's a man with a dark past—he's very attractive.

"They say he's from the underground," added Andrea, slightly lowering her voice.

But we didn't go to church.

For a while we were trying to discuss the incident with the soldier but it was hopeless. We decided to stop by a late-night café.

In the morning we woke up in the same bed.

A WOMAN AT THE
COSMETOLOGIST'S

She was on her way to the cosmetologist, deliberately creating trouble for herself. It was, I tell you, quite the case—a familiar case for many of her friends and not sad in the least. She hated cosmetology as a whole and every cosmetic procedure in its own right, but there was nothing she could do: she had to go to the cosmetologist the way some people have to go off to military service.

"What are you supposed to do," she would say to herself, "when there's no color in your cheeks, your face is sallow, tone off, and you're puffy and swollen? I am also, apparently, losing density." And so, hunched over, bowing her head like a sacrificial animal, she led herself to the cosmetologist—two blocks down if you turn right out her front door.

A massage table occupied the middle of the cosmetologist's small basement room. The woman always called it "the bed" to herself. And this bed easily lent itself to being hated and accursed in her heart. The bed stood as if intended for autopsies, and two glossy blades of medical lamps rose above it like candles. A thin, green-paper blanket lay over a white terry-cloth towel. It never looked like a fresh blanket, although at the beginning of every visit, right under the woman's eyes, the cosmetologist would cut a human-sized piece of fabric from a roll and make the bed with it. Thus all her clients enjoyed new bedclothes, yet the cosmetologist was free from the cares of laundry.

The bed was immersed in a cloud of odors, hovering over it and forming the dome of this temple of beauty. The cosmetologist's hands flitted to and fro beneath the cloud, like birds above a despoiled nest. The woman wasn't fond of these hands. There was something strikingly inadequate about them, dubious, as they moved in concert with each other. The fingers wriggled across her face, sweet and treacly aromas with hints of decay and baby powder penetrated her nose, two circular cotton pads were laid over her eyes and she turned blind.

The cosmetologist is a psychologist of sorts, the woman thought to herself. If I'm undergoing change, if I'm seized by anxiety or longing, or groveling before somebody, I can see her and ask her for help. She will not refuse me—she has never refused me.

It nonetheless remained unclear how to broach topics that lay perhaps quite far from the cosmetologist's occupation. How to speak about exhaustion that jars you awake in the middle of the night, or the fact that the warming heat of a realization travels along the body, like the soul in the conceptual world of the eighteenth century, migrating from the temple to the ring finger, alighting in turn on the arm, the kidney, the spine, and finally the heart.

The only language the cosmetologist understood—the woman knew this with a sure and certain knowledge—was the language of skin.

You can visit the cosmetologist whenever you feel troubled, but you must arm yourself with phrases like "My face is bloated," or "My skin is dehydrated, it lost its luster and is showing faint wrinkles," or else you must resort to such scientifically sounding expressions as "My epidermis is lacking in collagen again."

And the cosmetologist—so the woman was convinced for no apparent reason—will understand that these aren't mere words, but that they conceal mountain ranges of sobbing and deserts of heartache penetrating the body, like a small hungry animal too cute to be dexterously annihilated.

After everything the woman lived through over the past three years—this woman who was registered in Kyiv as a resettler, that is, a refugee—after the many free consultations offered to her, after empathetic eye-contacts with big-eyed psychologists inviting her to appointments and tendering their support, after the human rights activists who, in the opinion of the woman, were interested only in protecting the rights of women but not in her person, the woman, pulling herself together, decided that she had no other options but to visit the cosmetologist again.

Having called in advance, she descended the stairs to the basement unit. Spaces Not for Living Realty generally situated its units, which it rented out to numerous Kyiv beauty salons, in cold stuffy basements. "These really are not spaces for the living," thought the woman, "but for those wishing to leave life, albeit temporarily."

The cosmetologist appeared a little shaken, as usual. Acting against her own rules by not waiting for the client to take off her shirt and lie down on the massage table, she immediately started to stroke the woman's face with the palm of the hand, to lift her chin, and to touch her neck.

"How do you like my new cream? It helps, doesn't it?" The cosmetologist was expressing interest. "You have quite another face now, milky skin, no one would recognize you!"

"No, what are you saying?" The woman tried to exonerate herself. "Your cream helps, sure, but the dryness is becoming more conspicuous on the skin. It is settling deeper, it can't be hidden, it will not be suppressed."

The cosmetologist, voicing diverging opinions on the topic, forced the woman into a horizontal position and silence.

Then the woman saw the hands, the kind that evoked heavy memories in her, going as far back as kindergarten—hands with short, well-kept nails—scuttling their way to her face, while the voice, which might have been called infernal if it weren't extremely high, rang out from above, "Your face is so fresh, what a good girl you are."

Her words mingled with the manifold scents of the beauty salon: the smell of fusty skin, soap, perfume, and the awkwardly concealed meatloaf sandwiches that, prior to the woman's visit, the cosmetologist devoured in an attempt to assuage the subterranean hunger which always grew ten times more intense during work.

Beauty salons are, in their own way, war trenches and dugouts. Hungry soldiers hide in them, smeared with creams, injured by injections, ready to endure anything for the sake of anything.

The cosmetologist suggested that the woman relax. She lay on the massage table. Each touch of the cosmetologist's hand felt like a blow or a gunshot. Her skin was under bombardment; huge pores yawned open like the mouths of volcanoes. There was the murmur of water, the movement of cotton balls along the cheekbones, caustic lotion, dark blotchy fingers nearing and retreating, the piercing yellow light of the medical lamp directed onto her face.

Only here could she relive the most terrifying episodes of recent years—she could relive them again and not feel any shame for purportedly finding herself in safety.

What safety was there to talk about? The facial massage would pull her upper lip up like a lifeless growth; the caustic aroma caused dizziness and nausea; the contours of objects blurred because of how helpless she felt.

In this way—from contact to movement, from a wave of terror to a fit of shuddering—time slowly passed, each minute refusing its end, and the woman began to feel better.

The day after her appointment with the cosmetologist some acquaintances glimpsed the woman in the old botanical garden. You couldn't call the smile on her face "happy," but at least she was halting to admire the flowers.

THE SISTERS

A light, flowery scent: perfume. To start living, I frequently need to hold out till three in the afternoon, sometimes even to five. But it's almost evening already. The sun summons the stars to the sky, it summons its warrior host and hides behind the clouds. I am ironing clothes out of the wash, cleaning up this and that, and falling depleted into bed. Each day I have to start life anew, I have to learn to rejoice in each day gone by. Tell me this one very simple, elementary thing. I can't understand what morning is, how yesterday happens to flow into today. Today also has to vanish. From a certain moment on I totally lost my bearing and now I don't know what a beginning is. At some point each of us came to be. Rivers begin in a spring of water. Where is the start of my day? Usually I wake up tired. My sister sleeps in a bed near me. So as not to think about anything, she found a job where they pay her a salary. We weren't out of money yet. The work is highly remunerative. She washes dishes in the American embassy; sometimes she sets the table for dinner parties or brunches. The Americans are sympathetic to our misfortune. Sometimes they pass us clothes or, on rarer occasions, linens. We like to wear their clothes, especially those in sizes slightly larger than ours. It's pleasant having clothes on you that make you feel at home. A house never fits snug over the body.

A few journalists expressed interest in me. They wanted to know our story. But I couldn't tell any of them anything. Not so with my sister. She told our story to many listeners—not just journalists, but also directors, artists, actors. Then she got bored and began to tell the stories of our neighbors, the stories of our acquaintances, and eventually, stories that, she suspected, had no relation to our life at all. She passed these stories off as the troubles, wanderings, and misfortunes that we went through.

My sister likes to make things up. Sometimes I think of the war, the shellings, the deaths of people we knew as things she made up for her own entertainment.

She had nothing else to do. She got bored of the world that would, from time to time, hand her the habitual bouquet of flowers, so she made up convoluted, complicated tales to force someone to really listen to what she was saying.

Whatever. She of all people certainly had no need of making things up. She always had sycophantic individuals dancing attendance to her. They hung on her lips from the outset, always with pleasure, sometimes with admiration.

———

Each morning my sister—who is younger, prettier, more perfect, and superior to me in intelligence and willpower— gets up at six, brushes her teeth, lightly massages her cheeks to give them color, without fail puts on foundation and blush in case of an unforeseen onset of paleness, and goes to work. She always dresses with such effect that neighbors peer out of the windows to see her walk from the building entrance to the bus stop.

Home alone, I sometimes start looking for her.

When she's not there, I may look for her under the lids of pots, in frying pans, inside dressers, on the stove.

My sister arrives and tells me how her day went. She plays easy with the truth when she says she has never been in the company of such important people before. A certain man from the embassy, it turns out, volunteered to take her home and was extremely gracious. He spoke Russian as well as we do, although he was American. Quite an honor! Imagine that! Our family wasn't at the bottom of the barrel in our town, and we knew people more important than the ones who fill to overflowing the embassies of different countries in Kyiv.

They were risk takers, people who evoked admiration from us but about whose lives we knew next to nothing. They inspired fear, they were reckoned with, but it was hard talking with them, in fact, they practically didn't know how to talk. When they were in our company, they stayed silent and drank beer, or they exchanged a few rare words that we hardly understood, in reference to various plans of theirs beyond our comprehension. They were unashamed of their importance, and didn't hypocritically pretend to be just like everybody else, after the fashion of

most other embassy workers. I was envious of my sister
because they visited us for her sake, to be in her company.
But then we stopped seeing them. It happened after one
remarkable incident that I don't want to talk about. These
were wonderful people in their own way. Each one of them
was handsome. One had an elongated head and dandyish
leather bracelets and wristbands. On another's chest hung
a massive cross with a skull—symbolizing royalty, as he
explained.

My sister knew how to surprise me. Throughout my
whole life she served up surprises, shocking me again and
again by making new friends with people she could never
possess. Each was too big a beast for the likes of her.

And yet she is irresistible.

Formerly I could not tear my eyes away from her; now
I'm more used to her, maybe because I'm shortsighted.

Regular passersby used to idolize her. Her beauty was
authentic and indubitable. All men bowed their heads
in her presence, even the one who dumped her by the
drinking fountain for local water that we used to collect.
I remember how our priest arrived to bless this water.
He was dressed in black, like a monk. He sanctified the
water, and all the inhabitants of nearby houses started
coming to the spring. We, of course, thought that if we
were struck by misfortune, this water, holy water, could
probably save us.

My sister and I frequently strolled around this spring—
or rather around this drinking fountain by which a squalid
handful of old people usually collected—and imagined
Saint George rising out of the water. Of course he would
have a glowing golden sword in his hand, and be striking

enemies down with it. Not so much enemies as bad people who, as our priest often said, were basically possessed by evil spirits or rather were evil spirits incarnate.

We were practical adults, calculating and accommodating, but we managed to preserve a living corner of romance within. This is why we kept imagining these cute scenes.

My sister says that even now, while washing dishes in the American embassy, she half expects a wrathful Gabriel to arise out of the foam that fills the sink to overflowing because of the special detergents customarily employed in the embassy.

Everything, just everything in the embassy differs from our everyday life. Each object, each thing appears to be made for eternal use.

This isn't something you see in our reality, is it?

I think our entire reality, everything that, over the years, we've built, assembled, stacked, beautified is so easy to destroy, because we were doing it, are doing it, and will go on doing it while planning just one day ahead, or at best one week. There is nothing that we love more than what is temporary. Ephemeral, quickly spoiling, departing.

I am still astonished by the fact that we have a flag, an anthem, recollections of the past, songs passed down from generation to generation, like "Vannie, Vannie, leg it up," and "Where ya off to, Nata, huh?"

I think the time has come to systematize everything. Just make two columns: "for temporary use" and "for eternal use." Distribute everything, everything without exception, between the two columns, and then all of us, our society as a whole, must choose one of them—for example, in a referendum. As for the column not chosen, it can be destroyed or given to another country as a gift.

I also have a lot of other ideas.

PHILOSOPHY

As far back as 2014, when everything was just beginning, a Ukrainian soldier would tell me that he married war. He said, "I got married, imagine that, finally married. My parents were driving me nuts, they ridiculed me these past years, although I'm only twenty-six. They repeated, 'Look at yourself, you're going bald already, you're not at all the little boy we once loved. It's time!' They didn't even say, 'It's time for you to get married!' They just grumbled and lamented, 'It's time!' And I believed them, I did!"

He figured a way out of his pointless conflict. He decided to marry—he initially kept the thought to himself—not some woman but something else at once more significant and more serious. He was searching for a life goal that played to his strengths, and he found it. He married war. Or rather he did what almost all young Ukrainian men do. He took a wife he couldn't handle, who dominated him, demeaned him, and cheated on him. He got ahead of himself. He was in a hurry to marry, but his fate would not tarry, as he magniloquently put it. His parents calmed down somewhat. Their son settled down. It's amazing but he convinced them, too, that the wife he had found was the one they always wanted for him. What he liked about war is that it played hard to get. Once his company sat in dugouts for two months, but there was no war happening.

Wintertime, during constant shelling in the cold, they wouldn't drink despite feeling very scared. Scared during the day and at night—so scared that one of them, whom they called the Poet, could cry like a rooster or an owl for hours, but no one thought of making him shut up. Their unit was positioned near a township called Happiness and, at dawn, they teased the Poet: "Feel the happiness yet?" Their jokes were good-natured and never—you hear me, never—meant as put-downs. Soldier heroes, soldier cannon fodder. They talked about themselves with a touch of mockery, and the Poet wished for someone, anyone, to describe their gallantry in the same breath as their banality.

Drinking, they imagined that they made up two or three or even four warring camps. At first they sang songs, then they playfully thwapped one another, like infants in a nursery, then they would start fighting in earnest. They shouted: "Separatist, separate yourself!" "Ukie, go home!" And only after a few hours of such battling, which never resulted in casualties, would they fall into the sweet sleep of children.

———

War disarms? War takes away hope and meaning, makes everything grey, and sucks life out of the city and the street, leaving nothing?

What do you mean? War is a great help for us. It provides us with distraction from ourselves. It absolves us from seeing ourselves close up. It's been some time now that we've been peeking into ourselves through war only.

We hate ourselves. That's the problem. We hate any outcome of our public life, our activity. We even hate our own national culture, and so we can fall in love with it solely on the account of the afflictions, persecutions, and deaths that befall it.

Yes. No renaissance can take place in Ukraine except on the eve of terror and executions. We can't arrive anywhere—we love to be on the move, yes, we adore movement, direction, vectors. At the same time we are ready to easily trade one vector for another. But we aren't capable of arriving anywhere. As far as we're concerned, any terminus, any stop on the way is like our death.

So it turns out that war has begun but the catastrophe hasn't struck yet?

We don't smile as much, we do everything automatically without putting our heart into it, but there's no catastrophe yet. There's only the premonition of catastrophe. And that's good.

Because any premonition is better than any result?

Yes, because the acquisition of identity, the acquisition of—begging your pardon—a self is going to be the real catastrophe. We feel fine only if the thought hasn't been thought to the end, if nothing gets fully expressed.

LIGHT ATTRACTORS

On a dark winter night, in the middle of an empty street, you can see four lights. Each one is a street lamp, hung near the four corners of a small one-story building. If you know for sure that emptiness reigns in your soul, you must leave your house in the evening and head for these glowing fires that float near walls like hummingbirds before flowers.

In another moment you might decide that you will find rest in the unfamiliar building, or that here people will greet you with open arms and treat you to coffee and wine.

A myriad of things might pop into your head while you walk courageously, step by step, toward this unprepossessing toy of a building, as you overcome a significant number of empty footsteps and empty roads. Basically, you'll think that you're swimming in emptiness, although there will be firm soil under your feet. Someone else's thought, *This must be what the road to success is like*, will flash through your mind.

Finally you are at the doors. You catch fragmentary sounds of music. Of course the music was composed before you were born. Unknown people in other countries and other times have reached moments of happiness and abandon through its melodies. You don't pull the door open, you throw it open. Bravely, thinking you're a winner, you enter the building.

Then you halt in bewilderment.

Nothing happens, just like when you were outside. The music is inaudible now. It must have reached you through the open window of another building, or possibly never existed at all. Here it is as dark but slightly warmer as out on the street, and you sense someone might actually be waiting for you. Something about the air feels vernal. You walk through a narrow passageway into the neighboring space that has a coffee machine. You take a soft paper cup and place it on the shiny nickel-plated surface.

You hear how softly the water seethes on the verge of boiling. There are no chairs here, so you drink a small cup without sitting down.

In the unimaginably tender quiet you take the first sip. Then another, then another. You think that you've found the right path for yourself; answers to old questions rise up in your mind of their own accord; you've become better, more organized, and more attentive than you used to be. What else can be improved?

A delightful thought strikes you like lightning. You return to the dark passageway and find the window practically by touch. The narrow ledge is level with your chest. You pull up, opening the panes; the cold wind feels pleasant and fresh. Before leaping, you peer from the darkness inside the building into the other, external darkness, from one emptiness into the other emptiness.

Of course you don't die—it's a one-story building after all. You fly out and land smoothly on the ground. The happiest of moments, one you will frequently dream of repeating.

THREE SONGS
OF LAMENTATION

THE SNAKE

She crawled in anyway, the accursed one! Aimed for the heart and hearth, and entered right into our apartment, to check the documents, or so she said. Said she was from the social services and made right for the dresser with our dear drawers. So many drawers my old man built us, as if deliberately for such an occasion. How I wept ... how I wept! I wept for two hours afterward, or maybe four hours, I can't remember. She entered our room, our bedroom, which is also the living room, and went for the night stand, stood at the side of the night stand, and put her hand out for the documents. They lay in five packets, the documents, five multilayered packets. That's how we packed them on one occasion; I bent the corners of the packets with my own hands. She introduced herself as coming from the city's social services and said that we are getting special disbursements and because of that she needs to copy the documents. In my day I knew how to earn money, but a different time has come. And my old man knew, too—he was never shy about showing his mettle in things like that. Neither of us was a stranger to good money. As for drawers, we had drawers galore! Just for this occasion he had cut them, planed them, nailed them together. Or did we bring an old library card catalog home? I don't remember.

The borough library is shut down. Rain soaks books in cardboard boxes, the catalogs stand outside the entrance— why leave them to perish? Especially since such occasions have become more and more common. But my old man is a bit on the blind side now, and on the deaf side, too. He let her in. Let her have her way with the night stand, the dresser, the drawers. Were she a snake she'd be slithering her way out one drawer and into another. The drawers would be of great interest to a snake because there's plenty of places to slither. Were my old man a hawk, he'd have snatched the snake and carried her away. He'd have brought her to the nest. And the baby hawks would be waiting there, the wind whistling over their brown feathers; he'd see from high up how they'd open their baby beaks so wide for the bloody harvest. Why would they, the little ones, think the snake isn't food but something *living*—that she can think, she can feel? All they know is how to stuff themselves day after day. Stuff themselves and grow, grow and stuff themselves. And yet ... what if he were an old hawk? Being that he's old, my old man? He'd have had no kids, nor would he have managed to hold the snake in his beak. The snake would have fallen and smashed itself up on the rocks. Or else would have fallen onto a field and quickly slithered into somebody's hole, hidden in the high grass. You might as well seek the wind.

Still, from a hawk's point of view, he might be young, maybe even an adolescent, a clumsy devil-may-care youth, his whole life ahead of him! But she stole! Got in and stole! Carried two thousand out of the house. I'm in the metro, where you can't hear so well, and he calls me, saying, "We don't have our beloved two thousand anymore!" At first I didn't believe him. Then I rushed home, convinced myself, proved it. Opened up the small lower drawer, where the bills used to lie snug and warm under documents. There was either a constantly hot radiator next to them or a ray of sunlight from the window. Here, on this shelf was where they once used to lie, wrapped up for a rainy day, somewhat warm to the touch, kept warm by the heat from the outside. We have a gullible old man, yes we do. One day they whacked him on the head in the stairwell and made off with his bag. They saw he was a respectable man, and might be carrying valuables on him. He might be an old man, that man of mine, but he isn't a poor old man. Both of us know how to save up and where to keep the money. But that was five years ago. Whereas just recently, a week ago, they broke into two apartments on our floor in our building and took away everything valuable. The times we live in, what can I say, I just want to weep!

There was a man living above us; he was a big and strong man, gruff, serious, wouldn't say a word to you ever, but they got him, too. First they cleaned him out, and then they buried him right after that, took a collection for the burial, everybody living in our part of the building chipped in. So we were told we got off easy, my old man and I. Because we don't keep anything at home! He and I, we don't have anything. And even if we do, we don't keep it at home. And even if it's not at home we don't have it. It's better not to think about it, to almost forget about it.

LOVE

But who said they could fall in love with me? She loves me or she loves me not?

The other day I bought a suit for myself near Leo Tolstoy Square. Not many people in Ukraine have such a suit, trust me. Look from the front and the wool cleaves to the frame, emphasizes the body's natural shapes, lies smooth on the chest with never a crease by the shoulder, then the fabric falls precipitously to the wrist. People who've known how to count money since forever, whose pockets are full of the rustle of bills, who know how to tuck precious shirts into their pants, have never even dreamt of such a suit. Selection is something I'm good at. I always examine a thing from every side and notice what an ordinary person won't see. Others carry their wallets to wherever they're lured and unload immediately, as if in the confessional.

For me this suit isn't for holidays, nor for special occasions or meetings. I show up in it every morning at work, on the factory floor, with human resources, in the restricted office on the executive floor. It's a capital suit.

I always roll up in the Mercedes, one that expresses my status, obviously: S-class. I emerge from it full of energy, slightly disappointed but not without hope, usually arriving at work with machine exactitude by ten. I don't owe anyone anything, and I look at things with a pragmatic and practiced eye.

But she arrives at work by eight. Holds her purse by her side, pressing it close. All hunched over, wan. Wends her way with her head down, swaying sometimes as if she spent yesterday recovering from illness. Walks right over the grass, over our flower bed. You grow not only grass for these people, but flowers, geraniums, cockscombs, to add some culture to the factory courtyard, but they trample your efforts. I even thought of laying out an English lawn, but it would be a silly thing to do, because the workers can't stick to the asphalt; they insist on shortcuts. They're running late—apparently every minute of sleep is really valuable. So lazy. What can we have in common … Nothing surprises me anymore. She's worn out all over, down to the soles of her sandals. Doesn't have time to sew herself anything new, and only rarely buys a new dress at the market. You call that clothing? And she can barely say anything that makes sense anymore; she has no clarity of thought and she's lost her cleverness. I remember what a perky reasoner she was. But now she has her head in a spin, like the rest of them. Obviously she's thinking about bills day and night—electricity, water—how to afford school textbooks, how to prepare for the holidays. It's all highway robbery! One and the same thing spinning in your head, so you get dumber despite yourself.

By the way, I could have locked up this shop long ago. What do I need a factory for if it isn't profitable? And how much longer can a man work? There's no one else I can appoint as director, and I'm no worse at the job than others would be.

Still, there's some use to be got from our assembly line. Only at work, where there's no time to look aside, where they push you from the front or the back, and the quota piles up into the evening—only here does she forget herself. I have time to catch that special expression of hers as I make my way to the office. I walk between the rows and I can tell: she is immersed in her work, she sees nothing that happens around her, as if she were alone in the world, as if the fabric dust, thread, and scraps were like giant swaths of cloth, somewhat like clouds, and she is smiling at them. Or maybe she is smiling at me? It depends how you look at it. I did think through every detail of the line, and now everything goes in a circle, nonstop and according to my plan. No. The assembly line is a horrible, meaningless human invention. Maybe the most frightening invention. Surely nothing more terrifying has been thought up for a long time.

She's sewing the warp thread through but her partner is already pushing her in the back, like, hurry, sew faster: the partner is already done but *she is not there yet*. Or rather, she is there, she's an experienced worker, but the other one, who's ahead, still finishes twice as fast and now sits around with nothing to do, which means the quota might not be filled, which means going without salary if she keeps sitting around. So she hurries the one in front of her, and that other one rushes and makes a mistake. Now neither of them will go home. Mistakes are expensive, and it's hard to fix them. The partner, although she sews faster, really ought to sit still. No, she's restless, she wants to leave at 4:30 on the dot when her shift ends. Or maybe she secretly thinks she'll finish the quota early and go home at 4:00 today? Let's say I move her into the middle of the assembly, but she's worse at sewing that section, she's used to the warp thread—she's developed a feel for it. It's none of my business to move people around anyway. Let the foreman watch over them! You can't keep an eye on everyone ... but her work depends on the work of the one in front! Yet it also depends on her, on her initiative, personality, standards. So you get it on the nose, and receive the minimum wage you deserve!

On the other hand, tell me this, good people: how can she sew her front through if the other seamstress still hasn't passed the placket down the line to her? This thought alone makes me lose my mind. A thought that suffocates me, dries my throat. I almost can't find my breath. This entire operation rests on me alone! You can chop off your young hands, poke out your quick young eyes, but your partner isn't going to sew any faster! This partner of yours barely makes it to work, her legs dragging behind her, and after the end of her shift she has to stay for another hour just to finish the bare minimum. And nobody gives a damn about it, which is just and right, as they are working in synchrony with each other, one complete link on a common assembly line! And the reason the assembly-line principle has been implemented here is that I have a conscience—I am raising efficiency!

The system is elementary but it evades understanding. I am the one who arranged everything here, and yet I, like a schoolboy, continually strive to deepen my knowledge of the process. As an excellent example for you, outsiders, consider a certain six-armed woman. Quite tall but heavyish, approaching sixty. Lipstick (always), hair curled, remnants of red polish on her nails—an attractive woman; after all, it's been a while since I myself was a boy. And who cares if four of her hands work slower than the other two? Let's say that her four hands are more experienced—they don't make mistakes, their work is of higher quality. Still, it doesn't matter. Or perhaps it matters from a different point of view? I can't figure it out. And these are the kinds of questions I have to solve! That's my role! Nobody, nobody else can solve them. It goes without saying that the salary she receives is based on the speed of the labor of the four tardy hands. But there are also the other two, the agile hands! The nails on those hands are kept especially sharp to thread the machine faster. But can I orient myself in relation to them, can I lean upon them? No, I can't lean upon them, they're just too slippery, always covered in hand cream. Besides, the other four hands are more experienced.

I admit, it's not easy work. But in the end I don't need these people. I am sick of all of them. They always want something, they're never happy.

Big deal, I can do without the workers. People say: "Everyone dies alone." Perfect wisdom. Everyone is responsible

for themselves, that's what it means. Although maybe
it also means the contrary: Everyone is responsible for
others. However you look at it, or as we say, depending
which hand you start with. I don't want to die alone. An
extra month's salary, a bonus—I offered it all, the whole
world in the palm of my hand. Thirteen work teams
for one coat! And where's this world now? I prepared
everything, all the documents, fine-tuned the bookkeeper accordingly, organized the social policy of the
factory. A primary-care physician just for the workers.
Takes patients Tuesdays and Thursdays. Just make the
appointment in advance—call and say Vladimirovich
sent you.

But certain directors, contrary to myself, paint a completely different picture. Install sleeping bunks inside the
factory. So some workers are going to sleep while others
are just starting work. And vice versa, the latter sleep while
the former work. They have lunch and dinner here, in the
cafeteria, then take a short break in front of the TV. And
return home only on weekends.

   I considered all of these details and corralled everyone
into an evening meeting. "It's more profitable that way!"
I told them. But they just stared at me; I could sense we
weren't on the same page. I shouted, "I'll give you raises,
definite raises!" But they said nothing, gazed off into space,
not commenting. Once upon a time they came here: some
for a couple of months, some just to give it a try, then
they simply sailed along with the sewing stream. I, too,
sail along with the sewing stream. Maybe I'm ahead of
the current?

That's what they say around here when they know what it's like: That guy didn't come in off the street, you know, he did his time in the business.

THE GLORIOUS FEAT

I'm not going to complain, although my years give me the right. What of it, if the prices are going up—you can still arrange something or other to make up for the difference.

I've arranged things for myself pretty often and sometimes even very well. One time they asked me to care for a relative who was dying. She lay on a huge bed in a tiny one-room apartment, which she had decided to transfer to her ungrateful Kyiv grandchildren.

Who was I to them, I'd like to know, to just step in and take care of her? But that's not really the issue at hand.

She lay in bed, small and clean—thanks to my untiring efforts—staring at the ceiling, and preparing herself for the next world.

I stood next to her, to the right of the bed I think, tucked the bedsheets in, adjusted the pillow, and kept an eye on things.

Her children and grandchildren didn't feel any gratitude toward me back then. They wouldn't visit, saying they'd be arrested here in Avdiivka.

One evening—the very evening when my story takes place—the dying woman woke up and said to me in a tinny voice, "You go, go straight to the wardrobe where the books are, at the bottom there's a drawer with socks, take the white pair out and unroll them."

I figured right away that there might be something to it. Walked over to the case, thrust my hands in the drawer, and picked out the white socks. They had terry soles—high-quality, good socks. I unrolled them, and freed one from the other. Reached my fingers into the white pipe of the right-foot sock and pulled out a gold icon.

It was a heavy pendant with Holy Matrona offset in crimson. Everyone knows this holy saint never fails to grant success, happiness, and the fulfillment of secret wishes.

I stashed the icon into my pocket right away and returned to the bed of the dying woman. My relative lay with her eyes open and seemed to be thinking of something without taking notice of me. To check on *you know what*, I pressed down on her forehead with my index finger, but she still didn't notice. This aroused all kinds of thoughts in me but, on the other hand, there was the icon in my pocket. I considered generously passing it to her grand-children, although these grandchildren didn't visit their grandma even once but went on disbursing free advice from another city.

As I was in the middle of my thoughts, the window noisily creaked and then swung open. The room went dark, an icy gust of wind blew through it, and the nasty round phiz of the angel of death materialized on the windowsill.

Grey steam poured from his nostrils. His eyes bulged out under his forehead, which was lined with anxious wrinkles. I instantly placed my hand over my pocket where Matrona hid.

But he—he didn't go for my relative like he was sup-posed to. No, he lurched my way and put his hand over that very same pocket. His hand was pressing down on the pocket, feeling around for the icon. My hand, though, was also inside that pocket. That pocket of mine had been sewn on crookedly, and in a place, well, you don't need to think too hard to figure out where. Not a nice scene to be having next to a woman on her death bed.

So I wasn't letting go of the icon, but he was closing in on my pocket without so much as a word. I indicated with my eyes, Look! the old lady's having a final moment, but it's like he wouldn't see her, he was just sidling up closer to me, that son of a bitch. Every feather of his standing on end, eyes boring right into me. I don't know how long we wrestled. I took a step, he took a step; I bent to the left, he bent the same way. But I wasn't giving up. All of a sudden I saw that everything's disappeared a long time ago. I was standing by the stove in the kitchen, heating the teapot. My trembling hand flew for the pocket—the icon was there, hot and heavy. I ran into the room, and the old lady was sitting on the bed, looking for her slippers. That's how she regained her health.

Her grandchildren still didn't come over from Kyiv, but they were very pleased.

And as for the icon, they let me have it: Thank you, they said, for winning our grandma back from the Enemy.

At least they thanked me. That's the price I pay for the things I gain in my life. How can I not value them?

FOR EXAMPLE

The first of two real-life examples:

A certain young seamstress after a long time of pon-
dering—after years of preparation and of steady, diligent, and stubborn accumulation of funds—decided to
go to Paris. Of course she had dreamt of Paris her entire
life. And of course she had not the least real notion of
Paris. Nonetheless, her sometimes desperate persistence,
never before witnessed by her circle of friends, resulted
in her finding herself in Kyiv, where she had arrived from
Vinnytsia. She was on her way to the airport, with a fresh
visa in a new international passport plus a reliable ticket
for a direct flight to Paris. Her possession of a direct ticket
needs additional clarification as the seamstress did spend
several months considering whether she ought to pay extra
for such a ticket or whether it might be more reasonable
to take a more economical flight with a layover in Minsk.
This seemingly trivial question deprived her of sleep,
occupied all of her thoughts for a stretch of time, although
not a very long stretch, dried out her skin, frazzled her
nerves, and finally entered her nightmares, where a drab
and imposing Minsk border guard eternally banned her
departure from Minsk if she continued to persist in her
desire to fly on to Paris in particular. Her dizzying doubts
brought her to the point where, with tears in her eyes,
she chose the direct flight, reducing her Paris sojourn by
one day. The seamstress planned to stay in a modest but
decent hotel. The weeks before her departure were spent
calculating the outlays necessary for the trip down to the
smallest detail, including the cup of coffee that she would
drink at the Paris airport immediately upon landing. Is it
worth mentioning that all her meticulous calculations were
worthless, because she lived in the Vinnytsia Region, where

prices had nothing in common with Paris prices? During moments of despair, she imagined the latter as astronomically high and, during brief moments of self-confidence, as comically insignificant.

And so this very individual, a tall woman with an earnest and slightly incredulous look on her face, on the way to the airport from the Kyiv Central Station, when the taxi was practically pulling into the terminal for international flights, abruptly demanded that the driver stop where there was absolutely no stopping according to traffic rules, and when he, with a low, discontented grumble, did come to a full stop, she hurriedly paid him, threw open the door of the cab, jumped out, grabbed her little suitcase from the trunk, and, without a word of explanation, headed for the sparse forest planted on the side of the airport, her suitcase jerking above the grass.

The taxi driver wanted to say something, to raise an objection, but he realized just in time that he had already been paid, patted his fat wallet with his broad hand—the way you pat a beloved but spoiled child on the shoulder—made a U-turn and drove back to the city center, where a new ride waited for him.

Given all that transpired above, I have a few questions:

Where did the seamstress really go?

Why hasn't she been seen in her hometown since she came out of the taxi?

Might her entrance into the forest be regarded as a *sui generis* severance of the complex and numerous agreements she had made with herself for this trip? Or was the passage through the forest merely the necessary prelude to a trip to Paris, which did take place, with unforeseen consequences for the seamstress, and so we've lost all contact with her and know nothing more about her fate?

Then there's this example:

A man from Zhytomyr dreamt his whole life of a small cozy one-story house with a red-tile roof. Often, while strolling about town, or taking care of business that didn't require particular attention, he sang simple ditties to himself on the subject of his dream:

> My little home,
> Roof, shelves, ceiling,
> Silent sleepy home,
> Guests find you appealing!

Or else:

> You're ready, my sweet house,
> All of you already built,
> But you still don't recognize me,
> As if I were a stranger to you ...
> You will not escape from me,
> Try and climb up to the attic,
> Out the window, into my backpack,
> I'll catch you wherever you flee,
> And teach you to be with me!

The man seemed to have a talent for composing songs and inventing melodies pleasing to the ear, for the local inhabitants of Zhytomyr took to inviting him to weddings and anniversary celebrations so that he would sing for them his best songs about his "sweet home."

He didn't want to refuse anybody; he sang his songs to a wide audience, trying to make his voice soft, to not breathe loudly into the microphone, and to sway smoothly in rhythm with the music.

And the day arrived when some residents of Zhytomyr began to remark on one incredible regularity connected to the singer. Those for whom the man performed his songs, whether they were newlyweds or celebrating an anniversary, acquired a home. Moreover, it was exactly the kind of home that the man sang about: single-story, albeit not always with a red-tile roof. The house might appear altogether unforeseen—for some people it literally materialized out of thin air in the form of a sudden gift or chance inheritance. However, and this was apparent to everyone, the singer didn't acquire—contrary to the logic of the events—any home for himself, despite spreading the happiness of homeownership to so many.

After several fruitless years of waiting, he finally remarked on this outrageous injustice and decided to leave Zhytomyr forever, to move to Kyiv and get a job in construction and give up singing.

This is how Zhytomyr lost yet another one of its bards. And now no one will ever hear, neither at a party nor in the city streets, the unpretentious little song that went like this:

> In the house it is light,
> The house is no darkling wood,
> And you will not ever gripe
> That you're in it, gone for good.

THE ADDRESS, OR SKETCHES
FOR AN AUTOBIOGRAPHY

Applause in the hall, a frisson of delight runs along the rows, enthusiasts rise from their seats and clap, standing. She speaks, constantly altering the tempo of talking, as if hoping her staccato phrasing might hypnotize the public, who are ready to become disappointed in her at any given second.

Thank you! Thank you for your attention! Thank you for coming! I will not delay sharing my most important news.

I want to state right away that I'm very successful.

Successful in practically any undertaking, from handicrafts to career peaks, which I reach instantaneously, judging by ordinary notions of time. I am already at the summit when others—absorbed in deep meditations, tormented by doubts—have only managed to raise their foot over the first step. People cling to each other in small cafés with the hope that the time will come for them, too, to be brought their order. But I receive my drink first.

Needless to say, luck pursues me wherever I go. A lucky charm seems to hang over my personal life—I have moved from one impeccable marriage to another, even more sponsorial one. No, it wasn't a transition that came easy; there were certain worries; I was tying knots in my handkerchiefs. There was a day when I walked into our old school, went up to the gym on the top floor, where my former husband and I had met each other, and performed four hundred squats with a brief pause after every eight! Nobody can dare charge me with insensitivity after that. Time has passed and I realize that the emotional duress that inspired this caper was normal and necessary—the most elementary and inevitable support for harmony in a second marriage that was just around the corner.

My husband is handsome; he has leonine bearing; he is attentive, sensitive, and a wonderful expert in his trade. He is affluent and can afford any sort of distraction but he often refuses distractions for my sake so that I would feel neither envy nor suspicion that his pervasive care, within whose compass I live, has momentarily slackened or been diverted down another channel.

There are times when I stroll through the spacious rooms of our suburban house in the noble mood of perplexity. Of course I don't just have one house—I also own three large, new apartments in a cozy modern neighborhood that is commonly described as "residential." I should note that the number of apartments hasn't changed since my childhood. I live in one of them, and the other two remain uninhabited. It's always been like that in our family. We renovated the apartments after the most modern manner, bought Czech chandeliers, decorated the walls with red imitation-silk wallpaper. We even bought trifling collectibles—plates, spoons, forks—but naturally we don't live everywhere, but only stop by the other residences from time to time to watch a movie or receive guests.

This coincidence will no doubt shock you once you consider the mathematical meaning of life. The same exact situation hasn't changed since my early childhood and adolescence—three apartments filled with glittering cabinet units and the rarest armchairs, three gorgeous family residences, two of which were usually empty. But this is why we're gathered here today—to detect the mathematical meaning of life and realize its algebraic laws so as to start manipulating them. Isn't that right?

Let us continue. As it happens, I earn so much money that I never wait for a payday; I never notice the prices in jewelry stores. If there's a counter that beckons me, I slip rings over my fingers and pay with my card without a second thought.

As I look around the faces gathered in this room, I recall the employees of my firm. Alas, the situation described above cannot apply to most of these people, who happen to be angry, skinny, choleric personalities, looking for new employment day after day, a third moonlighting stint, so that at least three always scant sources of income bring in at least something. In turn, you cannot say anything of the kind about me, since I work at a single job for only four hours a day, nowhere close to eight! And that, too, has been the situation from my childhood. From then on, in kindergarten, school, university, an iron four hours and no more than four hours no matter what. You will say it's a habit, but I can no longer be satisfied with such an explanation. Plus I've gathered all of you here to strive for something greater, much greater. I firmly proclaim: I have no bones to pick with anyone.

What I still need to do is to identify the problem, the question, the excruciating doubt that overshadows the brilliant audit I've made of my life. This question may upset or embarrass some of you, but I have no desire to awaken your conscience, which must be sleeping at the moment, like an innocent child. Rather, I need your collective mind for the solution of the dilemma of my entire life, a solution likely to be the guiding star of my future development.

What is it like to be a successful person, the most successful person in a city populated by losers?

My voice is breaking, I'd like to scream, but in my social position this would be inappropriate, to say the least.

Look around you now: where did all of this come from? Underslept children in kindergartens with roofs fallen in; the old, repainted monument to Marx that they tried to topple for over a week; potholes in cracked asphalt in the streets; cheated investors; a closed theater and alcoholic actresses?

I'm listening for your answers. Yes, I'm listening. Listening.

Even though it is a completely useless exercise.

The loser will never say anything. He'll always lift up his eyes full of chilling rebuke, and cut you to the quick. Or else he'll shrug in perplexity—at best, your success doesn't concern him. Indifference: the scourge of our time, our society!

This morning I visited a small perfume shop that recently opened on our street mainly to please just me. As I was leaving the shop, I ran into a man in a fedora. This neighbor of mine has been in love with me, often smiling at me with adoration and, at times, rapture, while his tender, discerning gaze spoke more eloquently than his smile. But today he looked frightened and came up close to me for the first time. Naturally—and everyone here can understand this passionate impulse of mine—I expected to hear his confession. A confession I had divined from his gestures and smiles, and from how he always turned around to look at me after I walked past him with my regal gait. I would fix my scarf, pretend not to see him, and look up at the heavens, as if counting the stars in the daylight sky. And so, after many months of mutual smiles, the subtlest of hints, and barely noticeable movements of the eyelashes, he walked up to me, he addressed me ... And then what? Speaking in a clear voice, not too loud but not too quiet, he asked me for a little bit of money, clarifying that he required it *for a cup of coffee*. The insistence and detachment of his tone, which sounded otherworldly, threw me into a panic! I pulled out the first bill I could feel from my wallet; he snatched the bill and immediately, without lowering his gaze, disappeared around the corner.

Awakening! Despair!

Now only the thought of a long-awaited holiday brings me comfort. I won't hide it, I'm celebrated quite often. Take just anniversaries of various events—I have several of them each year, not to mention my birthday, the holiday devoted to my profession, and many more.

At the same time, there is an insensitivity, a greyness in the people around me. No, a loser can't be moved by anything! Nothing affects him! They're a hard-hearted people, losers, stingy, unresponsive, their grey rows promenading into the distance, each walker engrossed in his own thoughts. How downcast they are! It's as if these people surrounded me with a fortress wall, behind whose heavy locks I perish! Their handshakes, their gazes, even their kisses carry bites, jabs, injections.

Listen to me! If you still retain any crumbs of what I regard as the elementary human quality of mercy, I beg you to tear down this wall! Turn into winners, construct a ladder, at last, dig mines, dismantle the heavy stonework and find me. I wound up here voluntarily, I fought for it, I was making my way here step by step, but now the conditions have changed, the prison has revealed itself and becomes more and more ruthless every day. You won't be sorry! I am like those magical things that point the way in the dark forest to treasures that seem to have been buried forever. I resemble a well-chosen day to be born, an auspicious prediction in your horoscope or a runes-casting session, when after anxiety and unrest, after the horror of sleepless nights, you finally encounter the sun: the rune of victory, power, and influence. In the end, the insignificant bodily movement that must be performed for my salvation will pay off so many times that you will never be able to count them, you will be surrounded by prosperity on such a scale that you will never …

Here the address abruptly ends.

THE NAIVE WOMAN

She was so naive that leaves rustled on trees in the park near her home.

She was simple to such a degree that the city grew and developed, new buildings were built, and people near her died and were born.

Her ceaseless clumsiness resulted in her constant tripping and stumbling. But others also tripped and stumbled because the asphalt in her neighborhood was riven by fissures and cracks.

She and her ubiquitous smile didn't disturb anyone—you might encounter her smile anywhere and would forget it right away.

How we loved her. We were devoted to her! But it didn't preclude us from giving her an occasional beating.

Although we also knew how to feel sorry for her. We never felt as sorry for other people as for her.

She knew how to touch your heart, particularly on the days when we forgot the date of our last encounter with her.

There was also one special phenomenon connected with her. Every time she took a bath, one of the birds in the suburban park would start singing. And whatever this bird did afterward, other birds held this one bird in esteem so that some of the birds would fly up to the one bird and clean the bird's feathers with their thin beaks to make this bird appear neater.

A BRIEF DECLARATION
ON WAITING

I agreed to meet a longtime acquaintance of mine at the Golden Gate metro station despite the fact that she had been putting on supercilious airs with me of late.

Andrea would initially call me, then not call me for a week, then call me twice again, twice in an hour, and then not call for a month. But she put on airs in other ways, too. For example, once we were strolling around together and she flung at me, "Yes, yes, I remember your words, but they didn't make an impression." Can you imagine?

You can't get away with acting like that—it doesn't just vanish from memory. I remember how she and I were walking down the street one day. She was gazing somewhere above the treetops as if oblivious to my words, and then all of a sudden she interrupted me and declared, "This summer is so hot, you can't even breathe." Then she yawned, as if I hadn't been talking to her a second ago, as coherently, thoughtfully, and articulately as I always speak. How unbearable is the loneliness you can feel in her company! Of course it happens to me, too, sometimes, when I'm talking to myself and my interlocutor interrupts my thoughts with a random remark and I imagine she has interrupted our conversation whereas she only terminated my silence. But, I swear, this wasn't what happened then! How excruciating to suffer such injustice, especially when you know you've been speaking aloud while counting on the attention of a person with whom meetings are so rare.

What's more, there are times when we're sitting in a café and Andrea smiles at me but actually she's laughing at me.

Or when she walks right past me without saying hello, and later claims she didn't want to disturb me.

She also plays this trick. I tell her how I was looking forward to seeing her; she replies with a joke, and I laugh—not because I feel like laughing but because I'm overcome with shame and bitterness. She follows with a barb about my laughter, that it's screechy, or "Russian," or "Ukrainian." One day she told me that I had "the laughter of Lviv," without further explanation.

And yet, with the passage of time after each failed meeting, I agree to see Andrea again. The truth is that during the span of our friendship I actually got to know her well. She is generous, sometimes majestic in her kindness. One day, in front of my very eyes, she picked up a dead bird from the pavement and took it home to care for and revive. Such conduct offered me a measure of instruction that I tried to absorb.

It was her magnanimity that pulled me toward the location of our meeting. I arrived several minutes late to show her that I also knew how to be late but also without making her wait too long. Yet she wasn't there. What was I hoping for as I prepared for our meeting, calculating in advance the minutes of my late arrival?

I sat on the sun-heated parapet for a while. The verdant earthworks of the Golden Gate rose behind me. It was warm. People stood around in the dull rays of the sun; many of them would soon leave with those they had been waiting for. I hadn't noticed when twenty minutes had passed. Actually, half an hour had passed.

Among those who, like me, tarried by the little area in front of the metro exit, there were some remarkable characters. I don't think they were waiting for anyone.

What if I, too, were here only to pass the time? That would definitely save the pathetic situation I was in. Not only would I have not arrived earlier than my friend would but, you could say, I completely spurned our meeting, finding myself here because of other, immensely weightier business.

Not far from me, on the island in front of the glass doors, stood a man with several tall plastic sacks; he stood behind the sacks, as if he were lurking on the other side of a wide, low wall. He wore a shapeless grey suit that looked as if it were drowning him. Sometimes he leaned forward to shuffle small, carefully packed bundles from one bag to another. The bags were bright yellow and green. I might easily have been standing with the exact same bags.

To really place yourself in someone else's shoes, however, you have to learn the details, figure out, inquire:

What is the purpose of his presence near the metro? And how long will his presence last?

"Hello!"

His response was pretending not to hear me, so I repeated:

"Hello!"

"Yeah, hello," he muttered, speaking almost to himself.

"I like the fact that that you're not waiting for anyone here."

"What?"

"Or are you waiting for somebody?"

"I don't understand."

"I guess I'm interfering in somebody else's business but I would like to resolve an issue having to do with waiting. How can I best explain it to you? You're standing here, by the metro, you don't need anybody, you're simply passing your time here, so to speak. Still, you look as if you do have somewhere you could be going to. You have many bundles with you, you don't strike me as a poor person. You're not a child, you have a family. Perhaps you're a brilliant master of a respectable profession, and your colleagues are waiting for you at your job even at this evening hour, since you're irreplaceable. But nonetheless you chose to come here, to spend time here, out in the open, on this windy, not very clean square. The whole world lies before you but here's where you've come to stand, alone, without complaints about your fate, without so much as a murmur, nor much glancing around, really. It can't be said that you're here to observe any incidents or to examine the passengers of the metro as they hurry home. You don't look at the couples in love, you don't give women any notice. This is the very reason why your figure, your confident posture, possibly, and your unspoken views all pique my interest. So I would like to know what brought you here. Please spare me no details. Probably not a personal relationship but a *waiting for a miracle*, yes, waiting for something unknown and mysterious?"

"I see how well you have divined my secret. For the first time in my life I've met a person who understood me without words, grasped me at one glance. I do come here sometimes, several times a week, to stand by the metro exit without waiting for anyone. Only here do I have the time to think about everything I've wanted to think about my whole life, but put off for later. It's the only place where I can be myself, indulge in the most free and unrestrained fantasies, and nobody will block my way, nobody will figure out what I'm really doing here. Lately, I confess, I've no longer wanted to waste my time in front of the metro on such thoughts, however momentous they may be. I am here, a part of my body touches the sidewalk through the soles of my shoes, my gaze is mainly directed toward a single point, although occasionally I turn my head a little like this and then return it to its original position. The most incredible visions appear before my eyes when I stand by the metro: unimaginable, astounding things become visible. Whereas trivial, everyday things, on the contrary, disappear from my field of vision, dissolve somewhere at the periphery, in the darkness. Eventually there always comes a particular moment—and I never leave before the moment arrives—when these bags that you can see standing before me, these huge, colossal, colorful sacks full of every necessity of life and even death, everything

I need for the most profitable of my deals and the best
of my sales, when they, these most common receptacles,
begin to glow. At first with the muted yellow glow of a
normal lightbulb; later with an astonishingly clean, white
LED fluorescence, marvelous in its perfection and rich-
ness of nuance. And only when that happens, when the
light begins to pulsate slightly in what may be described
as a frenzy, do I understand that I may walk away from
here—or else remain here for a bit longer to wait for
the events that follow, events I anticipate with fear and
bewilderment and cannot help but make wild guesses
about. Today, for your sake, I violated my essential rule,
the rule of *absolute*—I am not afraid to say it—*crepus-
cularity*, which is how my friends describe this state. But,
I very much beg you, please allow me to return to this rule
immediately. Honestly, I cannot spare you another minute,
notwithstanding your discernment that touched me to the
core. You must go away from me, even if you are the sole
person on Earth who could possibly share this state with
me, even if you alone are capable of understanding both
my immense joy and my initial fear. Still, I cannot allow
myself the slightest risk of losing this evening. To be sure,
quite possibly—I cannot fully exclude the probability—you
are not at all *this kind of person*—you never have been
and you will never learn to be."

TRANSLATOR'S AFTERWORD

The writer of this book is a photographer. She came to writing from photography, and she came to photography from political activism. She is a photographer who uses documentary methods. Each of her photo projects* explores a different community of people who are, literally, underrepresented. Her photographs are often accompanied by texts that register, directly or indirectly, how the subjects of the photographs talk about their lives.

Brick Factory Tour, one of her earliest photo series, looks at a brick factory manned mostly by women in an economically devastated part of West Ukraine. There are shots of women working and also shots of the environment they work in. The men are away doing migrant labor abroad, and are "anyway less able to bear

---

* The photographs can be seen at http://belorusets.com/

the repetitive physical strain of loading the kilns," say the women. Some of the photographs critically recall Soviet-era images of female industrial labor. An accompanying text narrates how Yevgenia Belorusets chanced to visit the factory, how workers in the factory reacted to being photographed, and how they conceive of their work, their employer, and the deindustrialization of their area which followed the demise of the USSR. "You'll take your pictures here and then they'll close the factory because of it.... Five villages will be unemployed again because of you," insists one of the women. The essay also considers the acute differences between the author's memories of the visit and the photographs as its material remnants.

Other vulnerable communities of Ukrainians documented by Yevgenia Belorusets include the inhabitants of a building declared "unfit for habitation" in central Kyiv, LGBTQ+ families across the country, and Roma settlements targeted by the far right. She photographed Maidan protesters during the revolution in Kyiv in late 2013 and early 2014. After Russian-supported separatist militias opened hostilities in East Ukraine, she entered the conflict zone to photograph and interview coal miners and other civilians surviving in the shadow of the fighting. Her multimedia installations, such as one on the dismantling of Communist-era monuments after the Maidan Revolution, explore the ideological unease of Ukrainian history-in-the-making.

Lucky Breaks, her collection of stories about women affected by the war in East Ukraine, draws directly on her experience as an artist. For example, her installation about mortar fire, *The Eye and the Sun*, documents a visit to the town of Debaltseve two hours before the daily bombardment was expected to begin, and an exchange she had with a local woman about basement bomb shelters. This installation looks ahead to her story "The Stars," in which residents of a city under fire venture out of their basement shelters at times suggested by the horoscopes in the local paper. The aspects of the story that may strike readers of the translation as fanciful—for example, that the besieged city is safe at particular hours for particular astrological signs, or that it is under attack by Canada—will be recognized by the readers of the original as beliefs some inhabitants of the former Soviet Union might easily entertain.

Many stories provide glimpses of the author-narrator, although they are always about somebody else and nothing gets said about the narrator as a person. Rather, narrator sightings serve to dispel the trope of authorial omniscience by framing each narrative as one in which knowledge of people and events is piecemeal and perspectival. Some stories bear the features of testimony-taking encounters where the narrator's contact with the protagonist recalls that of an ethnographer with an informant. It is the informant who is the point of attention, and it is the informant whose story and point of view the narrator attempts to represent. Unlike in traditional ethnography with its claim to objectivity, the informant talks back, especially in the three stories with (or without) Andrea. Placed at key points of the collection, these three stories focus on the main artistic and ethical problem Belorusets confronts in both her documentary photography and her fiction: the problem of representing somebody else. It is a problem that necessarily arises from reflection on epistemological finitude.

The term "fiction" in contemporary popular culture suggests the opposite of a "true story." In an interview occasioned by the release of *Lucky Breaks* in Ukraine, the journalist Tetiana Bezruk points out that the book "combines fictional and real women's stories," and presses Belorusets on the ethics of obscuring the line between record and invention in the age of fake news. The author's reply compares the truth of her fiction with that of documentary photography:

> Any document is partly a lie, and this is especially true of documentary photography, which only ever conveys a small part of reality. When we look at the world, we should, on the one hand, always believe a document, because this belief lies at the heart of our political position, our ability to act: we believe the document and it spurs us into action. On the other hand, we must, unfortunately, remember that any document is part of a subjective perspective on a situation, and may indeed be subjective to the point of absurdity.*

Lucky Breaks includes two photographic series: *But I Insist: It's Not Even Yesterday Yet* and *War in the Park*. It is not always clear which photograph belongs to which series. The series do not illustrate any event in the

---

* Tetiana Bezruk. "'We can't use the war to justify anything': photographer Yevgenia Belorusets on documenting Ukraine's most vulnerable groups." openDemocracy. November 6, 2018.

text but rather unfold separately. They help convey the kind of world in which the stories take place, and some of the moods that color it. Their inclusion drives home the deep similarity of the art of the writer with that of the photographer critically employing the documentary method.

The initial note before the preface to *Lucky Breaks* argues that photography does not register a preexisting reality but rather composes a reality from traces of artistic intrusion into everyday life. But the photographer does not call the shots. Belorusets likens her stories to photographs because both have "acquired the ability ... to escape the author's final control over past events, encounters, conversations, histories." There is a material stubbornness to each artform that prevents a line from being drawn between "truth" and "fiction" in any conventional sense of those words. Hence the stories constantly call attention to themselves as *stories*, as tales, as the manufacturers of conviction by narrative rather than logical or evidentiary means. What are the grounds for believing an individual tale, in absence of other evidence? The narrator's admissions of ignorance, the doubling of the preface, the frequent metanarrative reflections or digressions, and— most importantly—the layers upon layers of irony, but real irony, not the kind where the reader and the author know better than the character, all betray the book's preoccupation with the principal question of so-called fiction, namely: "What is truth?"

The job of *Lucky Breaks* is not to report on any particular true story, argues Belorusets in her interview with Bezruk. Rather, the book has a more abstract and general aim: "to re-establish the right of suppressed, unseen and unheard stories to be told." Testimony of subjective, traumatic experience is often marked by self-contradiction, ambivalence, and other rhetorical features that provide logical ground to dismiss it as unreliable, unverifiable, or simply untrue. For Belorusets, the silencing of subjective, traumatic experience especially affects women's voices.

Lucky Breaks is a deeply feminist book. It is feminist in a matter-of-fact but at the same time very assertive way, simply by having a woman speak about the experience of women—and to speak about it without self-consciousness, as something self-evidently normal. It is also a book that cares about class. Its protagonists are "ordinary" women, which is to say people who are not blessed with advanced degrees or economic comfort. Belorusets treats their stories and voices with utmost respect, even when they make claims or profess values that are probably at variance from those of the author. Above all, *Lucky Breaks* is a book about the effect of undeclared and covert military conflict on civilians—and especially on refugees, about the loss of place, social network and social status they suffer, and about the traumas they are unable to articulate.

The fighting in the East Ukrainian region of Donbas, where Russia supports separatist militias with special ops and disguised regular troops but presents itself as a nonparticipant, casts a shadow of unreality over all of *Lucky Breaks*. The war is invisible in the everyday life of Kyiv. Trade and travel continue between the two countries. Russian propaganda efforts and planted rumors cast the conflict in deliberately absurd and atavistic terms, not just to appeal to the emotional associations of Soviet childhoods, but to sabotage the very possibility of an independent truth. Thus, the epistemological questions posed by the stories may themselves be a translation of their subject matter. *Lucky Breaks* narrates the lives of its protagonists with the perspectivism, fragmentariness, and, above all, uncertainty that characterize the war as perceived by participants willing and unwilling—especially this war, which often feels as if no one actually knows who has been fighting whom. Some stories take place in the war zone, while others are set in the regions occupied by the separatists, often almost imperceptibly so. (Readers who look up the place names—and sometimes the last names of people—will have a better sense of the narrative.)

Even more stories concern women who fled from the war and are leading lives out of joint in Kyiv. Such is the story whose protagonist obsessively abandons and retrieves her broken umbrella: she talks to the umbrella as if it were a sick relative whose infirmity kept the caretaker in the combat zone. Such is the story of the woman who cannot abandon her thoughts of the apartment she had to abandon, or of the woman who medicates herself with visits to the cosmetologist. Even "Transformations," the story of the refugee who learned to transform small everyday objects into other small everyday objects, may be interpreted as "about" refugeehood and trauma at once. And in some stories it is impossible to tell whether the protagonist is a refugee or whether she is displaced in another manner.

Although—or since—they are set in a state of instabil-
ity, many of the stories are laugh-out-loud funny. There's
the touching narrative of Malvina, who tells God her
name is Martha and prays to him that he may make her
sick; she has no other vocabulary with which to think
about divine grace except that of having a caring, wealthy
boyfriend. Another medieval-style miracle tale is that of
the caretaker who wrestles with the angel of death. The
seer of dreams beholds panoramas of ancient Ukraine,
where dinosaurs graze alongside elephants in saddles
decorated with folk embroidery. In another dream, the
seer gets down on all fours to drink blood and feels
herself "turning into a completely different person—a
European, an inhabitant of a great and ancient land."
(The most prominent of many allusions in this image is
to underworld shades in the *Odyssey*, who attain cogni-
zance of their surroundings only after drinking sacrificial
blood. Freud compares them to repressed wishes.) What
is so funny in Belorusets's depiction of how characters
think is their mental fusion of contradictory religious,
sexual, political, and pop-culture clichés. What is admi-
rable about her characters is that, despite the clichés,
they nonetheless act of their own volition and preserve
their dignity.

The two writers to whom Belorusets is most indebted
are Nikolai Gogol and Daniil Kharms. Gogol's representa-
tions of lower-class Ukrainians in his early stories, his
normalization of the supernatural, his Romantic concern
for the elements and fictionality of narrative, his play with
different discourses and, above all, his comedy, stand at
the origins of the writing of *Lucky Breaks*. The author's

approach to narrative is also inspired by the Russian writer Kharms. The telltale Kharmsian motifs of the miracle and the disappearance haunt her book. Her understanding of narrative is informed by the Kharmsian concept of the story as *sluchay*, incident, event, or, sometimes, random occurrence. The figures that translated Kharms's reactions to violence in Soviet society now help to reflect on life during the covert war in the Donbas.

The language of the book is Russian, except the first preface, which was composed in Ukrainian at the request of her original publisher. Russian is a controversial choice for a Ukrainian writer both politically and logistically. Ukraine is a country where almost everyone can speak both Ukrainian and Russian, and many people get to use both languages daily, although Ukrainian is by far the main language in, roughly, the western and central parts of the country, whereas Russian is more common in the east. A lot of language mixing take place, both within the bounds of a single conversation, and within the village dialects spoken by millions, called *surzhik*, that have no written form. But most Ukrainian citizens who care about language would like Ukrainian to become the one language of the nation.

The presence of so much Russian on Ukrainian territory is the linguistic consequence of colonial history. During the Imperial and Soviet periods, the state made efforts to suppress the use of Ukrainian as an autonomous language of culture and politics. The areas of the country emptied during Holodomor, the Soviet-made terror-famine of 1932–1933, in which millions of Ukrainian speakers starved, were resettled with Russian speakers from elsewhere in the Soviet Union. The last major Ukrainian poet to suffer captivity, Vasyl Stus, died during a hunger strike in a Soviet labor camp in 1985.

However, Ukrainian and Russian also have a long history of coexistence. They emerged from the same medieval dialect continuum that had its literary and political center in Kyiv, not Moscow. After their separation, Russian language and literature were often influenced by, or simply made, in Ukraine. Graduates of Kyiv's Mohyla Academy were crucial in the early efforts to Westernize Russian culture. The great Ukrainian Neoplatonist Hryhorii Skovoroda composed poetry and philosophical prose in a fusion of Ukrainian, Russian, Church Slavic, and Latin that stylistically recalls Robert Burton and Sir Thomas Browne. Nikolai Gogol, so far the only Ukrainian writer known worldwide, worked in Russian, even when composing his early stories about Ukrainian villagers that draw on Ukrainian folklore. In the twentieth century, "Russian" avant-garde and modernism can be described as largely Ukrainian and Belarusian, especially if one includes the Jews, most of whom, under the Empire, were allowed to live in Ukraine and Belarus but not in Russia. Even some late Soviet and early post-Soviet Russian-language poetry was written by poets who grew up in Ukraine and considered the literature and art of Ukrainian Baroque to be among their formative influences. As for the poets of modern Ukrainian, they were aware of and often in dialogue with Russian poetic developments as well as Polish ones.

The Ukrainian census of 2001, the only census to have been conducted so far on the territory of post-Soviet

Ukraine, counted 67.5% of the population whose native language is Ukrainian, and 29.6% of the population whose native language is Russian. (The ratio has certainly shifted in favor of Ukrainian since then.) This statistic exposes a number of ideological biases that are wildly off the mark in a bilingual environment, such as the assumption that each Ukrainian citizen has one native language rather than two or more, and that the native language is a clearly and institutionally defined "national" language rather than an intermediate dialect such as *surzhik*. Furthermore, the census relates language to ethnic identity, which is also considered in exclusive, rather than multiple, terms: you can only have one native language and one ethnicity.

As a result, the language issue is a heated one in political life. The Russian Federation has mustered its internationally popular but state-controlled media to present Russian speakers in the former Soviet republics, including Ukraine, as oppressed ethnic minorities in need of protection from the Kremlin. Ukrainian political and cultural leaders, on the other hand, regard their national language as under threat from Russian, a language given access to a much larger cultural and economic market. Hence, many Ukrainians see bilingualism as a situation where Russian would make gains at the expense of Ukrainian. The parliamentary law of 2012, recognizing Russian as a regional language, met with much controversy and even minor violence. Russia took advantage of the law's repeal during the Maidan Revolution in order to summon the specter of linguistic discrimination for propaganda purposes during its seizure of Crimea and covert invasion of the Donbas

Region. Although Russian-speaking Ukrainians have not, in general, been sympathetic to the Kremlin, but instead have volunteered with the Ukrainian Army in the east, the new language law of 2019 considerably diminished their language rights in comparison with the law of 2012. Russian intervention has also made Ukrainian cultural elites—even those who speak Russian at home—more determined to have cultural life in Ukraine take place in Ukrainian.

On a practical level, this aspirational monolingualism limits the opportunities of Russian-language Ukrainian writers to publish and be read in their home country in their working language. Instead, they are encouraged to switch into Ukrainian—a transformation likely to flatten their style and reduce their capacity for nuance. Alternately, they can seek publishers in Russia; however, books published in Russia cannot easily find readers in Ukraine, since they are not carried by Ukrainian bookstores. Belorusets is currently not willing to publish in Russia. As a Ukrainian writer writing about Ukraine, she wants to be published and read in Ukraine. Her language is subtly different from the kinds of Russian spoken in the Russian Federation; it is based on the rhythms and intonations of the Russian of Kyiv and Kharkiv, and continues the Russian-language line of Ukrainian literature.

I have given the place names in this Russian-language book as transcribed from Ukrainian rather than from Russian (Kyiv rather than Kiev), because I think Ukrainian forms are increasingly becoming the standard in English. I also stick to Ukrainian names for regions in the conflict zone, which are more Russian-speaking. I make an exception only for locations with telling names, like the Soviet mining towns Antratsyt and Marhanets, which I call "Anthracite" and "Manganese" to remind the English-language reader why these cities exist in the first place. Perhaps that exception is misguided; however, many of the region's place names have meanings that I can't bring myself to erase by transliteration. Ironically, some of the most brutal fighting in the Russo-Ukrainian War took place in the township Shchastia, a name that means "Happiness" in both languages.

The typical sentence in Belorusets is based upon the comma splice, as is also the case with some other writers of her geographic and/or political background. The comma-splice sentence tries to register the tonal, rhythmic, and semantic strategies of speech, and it may perhaps be interpreted as a gesture of resistance to the standards of correctness upheld by the apparatus of the Russian state. Unfortunately, the comma-splice sentence is currently felt to be a violation of the linguistic standards promulgated by American literary and educational institutions. American conventions also demand much more explicit marking of causal relations than was carried by the suggestive parat-actic sentence structure of the original.

The book's critical attitude toward plot—and its take on the sensation of time in general, especially in the regions of political and cultural periphery—appears on the syn-tactical level in how often verbs assume the imperfective aspect, which English lacks. I did not manage to put as many verbs as I would have liked into the past continuous tense, or to otherwise make up for the imperfective to the extent I desired.

Lastly, the Russian title of *Lucky Breaks* is *Schastlivye padeniia*, or *Shchaslivi padinnia* in Ukrainian, meaning *Happy* or *Fortunate Falls*—or rather *Fallings*, since the plural noun emphasizes the process at the expense of the result.

EUGENE OSTASHEVSKY

BERLIN, JULY 2021

ACKNOWLEDGMENTS

The author wishes to express her gratitude to Aleksandr Cherkasski, Katja Petrowskaja, Ivan Melnychuk, Nikita Kadan, Lada Nakonechna, Martin Pollack, Patrick Evans, Nelia Vakhovska, Claudia Dathe, Tatiana Ushkats, Elena Vogman, Natalia Chemalykh, Kyrylo Tkachenko, Mark Belorusets, Alla Zamanska, Pavlo Lissianski, Dmitry Galkin, Daria Kuzmich, Alina Kleitman, Dana Kosmina, Eugene Ostashevsky, Katerina Nosko, Uliana Bychenkova, and Katharina Raabe.

She also would like to thank Tatiana Baskakova for editing the Russian text of *Lucky Breaks*.

The work on the original book was supported by the Grenzgänger Program of the Robert Bosch Stiftung and the Literarisches Colloquium Berlin.

The translator would like to thank Daniel Medin and Jeffrey Yang.